Barl

The true story of
Maria de la Torre

As told by
Brandon Royal and Paul Strahan

SNP·EDITIONS

an imprint of

SNP·INTERNATIONAL

Based on the true story of Maria de la Torre as told by
Brandon Royal and Paul Strahan.
Although this book is based on a true account, the names of
persons, places, or things may have been changed and should
not be interpreted as factually or historically accurate.
The authors may be contacted at
GPO Box 440, Central, Hong Kong or by email at
bars_of_steel@yahoo.com

Published by SNP International
A division of Media Asia Pte Ltd
491 River Valley Road
#01-19/20 Valley Point
Singapore 248371
Tel: (65) 6826 9600
Fax: (65) 6820 3341
http://www.snpcorp.com

Printed and bound in Singapore by Utopia Press Pte Ltd

ISBN 981 248 003 X

National Library Board (Singapore) Cataloguing in Publication Data

Royal, Brandon, 1967–
    Bars of steel : the true story of Maria de la Torre as told by Brandon
Royal and Paul Strahan. – Singapore : SNP Editions, c. 2003.
    p. cm.

    ISBN : 981-248-003-X

1. Torre, Maria de la. 2. Prostitutes – China – Hong Kong – Biography.
I. Torre, Maria de la. II. Strahan, Paul. III. Title.

HQ253
306.742092 – dc21   SLS2003003776

Contents

Prologue *5*

1 Simpler Times *7*

2 Dark Clouds *18*

3 Green Seas *35*

4 Baby Butterfly *49*

5 Deep Waters *59*

6 Eyes of the Night *73*

7 Grey Puffs of Smoke *81*

8 Bamboo *103*

9 Mud Slide *124*

10 Barking Dogs *129*

11 Mangoes, Ripe for the Plucking *144*

12 Clearer Days *160*

13 Bird Garden *170*

14 Recipe *190*

Glossary *197*

Prologue

When a typhoon arrives in the hot tropical months of a Philippine summer, wind and rain join forces, breaking bark and bending steel. Whereas water can carry debris, erode rock, and cause mud to slide, wind is nature's invisible force, to be felt but not seen. The real measure of a typhoon's strength is not the highest signal posted by the weather station at the peak of the storm, or even the storm's duration, but the actual damage caused by its passing.

Youth is but a water- and wind-filled storm—the more forceful and dramatic are the formative events, the more distinctive will be the remnants that mark its aftermath.

1. Simpler Times

To the casual eye, the barrio landscape contained no clear divisions. Fences were seldom used to separate one half-brick, bamboo house from another and chickens and dogs wandered freely in the open spaces and along the dirt road. Colours of green, brown and grey merged as patches of grass and flattened dirt gave way to rice fields and stretches of vegetation. The way in which one area flowed into the next and the lack of clear visible boundaries was perhaps an unremarkable feature, but one that most defined the barrio landscape.

AT SIXTEEN I was the second eldest in my family by just a year, and although my elder sister could equally have left to find work overseas, she instead suffered another of the disasters that seem to plague many of the young girls living in the province. She found herself pregnant, having lost her virginity to a friend of the family who, incidentally, was married with four children of his own.

Both my sisters and I were brought up as good Catholics, like most of the families in the Philippines. We would proudly display our purity during the various religious festivals. Our white veils, kept from our first communion, would be washed, bleached and clipped to our neatly tied-back hair before we took our place at each procession. This purity was expected in young girls and we were taught to protect our virginity through to marriage. Much later I would recall those early days, and it would strike me as sad that our parents spent years bringing us up to protect our innocence, then endangered this innocence because they themselves lost control of their lives, both because of family size and lack of financial resources.

To this day I still do not quite understand what happened with my sister. She was a model of virtue. Never a flirt—quite the opposite—and even though we talked, as young girls are bound to do, of boyfriends and sex when we were in bed together and our younger sisters were asleep, I never dreamed she would actually do it. I am not sure that even she knows how everything evolved into the final mess. Was it curiosity or was she seduced by trust because he was a good friend of our father? The first real touch? Who knows? She did tell me later that he had often remarked how grown-up she looked, how he would stop to talk to her when they passed each other on the road.

It happened while my father was away. He had managed, through a friend, to get some short-term work from a transport company, driving a truck between Baguio and Manila. Baguio, Manila's summer capital, is situated in the mountains and eight hours north by truck from Manila. The drive was a strenuous one. The further north from Manila, the worse the condition of the roads. This just added to the stress for both driver and truck. In some places, where the road began to zigzag up through the mountains of Baguio, concrete had broken and was worn away. The holes were simply filled with small boulders and gravel, adding to the discomfort. Most drivers would try to time their journey up these mountain roads to daylight hours, for other than these potholes, many of the steep, twisting corners did not have embankments. My father would drive the truck up to Baguio during the harvest season, pick up the vegetables and then drive them down to the dealer in Manila.

The altitude of Baguio offered a cooler climate and farmers were able to produce a larger quantity and better quality of fruits and vegetables, which commanded a high price in the cities. For the merchants and their trucks, the first to get their load to the markets could expect a good price. For those that arrived later in the day the reward was still good, but by no means as much as for the speedy and better organised. To be first to market also meant a bonus, and so the "vegetable race" would be played time and time again with each truck driver trying to outdo the other.

Cabbages, broccoli, green beans, cauliflowers and salad plants such as lettuce, cucumber and succulent red tomatoes would be packed into boxes and rushed to market overnight or in the early hours in order to arrive fresh. Delicate fruits like strawberries, which could not be grown elsewhere and were almost impossible to import successfully, were worth the effort. If farmers were willing to chance that season's weather, the fruits were in great demand and affordable to the rich.

My father would spend three or four days on the road at any one time. We were never sure when he would return home. The trucks were old and not well maintained and the constant struggle to drag the load up and down the twisting mountain roads took its toll on the noisy, old diesel engines. Even the mad dash from the nearby city of Angeles down to Manila on the relatively flat expressway was fraught with uncertainty. On one occasion, the axle of my father's truck snapped and he waited almost all day before it could be towed away for repairs. Two days later he resumed the journey, but by now with a load rotting from the heat and only fit for pigs. When he did eventually get back, he was in a foul mood—no bonus, hungry and tired.

For my sister and me, these trips gave us a little extra freedom. We would not be expected to be at his beck and call. All my brothers and sisters were a little frightened of my father. Even my mother was quiet and submissive, which is why I think she ended up with seven children. He was the boss in all departments. When he was away, my mother let us spend more time with our friends. For me, that was great. I could disappear and talk and play with my school friends. For my sister, who was no longer at school, it meant that she would help my mother with the daily chores, visit our grandmother and help look after the little ones.

One day, so I learned afterwards, my sister was coming back from our grandma's, which was only some three hundred yards further up the road, when she met up with our father's friend. They talked as they made their way back to the house. What they spoke about, my sister never told me, but they ended up in a friend's house, where some of the other men were playing cards. Playing cards is a favourite pastime of unemployed Filipino men. She joined in the talk and helped by pouring the beer. At one point, he followed her into the kitchen to help break a block of ice used to cool the beer. Few houses in the province had a refrigerator and it was a common sight to see young girls breaking the large blocks of ice bought from the local store. He put his arms around her from behind and gave her a squeeze. She did not react, but he turned her around and gave her what she described as a real kiss. Her hands were wet from the ice, but she found herself kissing him back. Then a moment after, he squeezed her waist again and returned to the card game. When the game was over or he had run out of pesos, he finished his beer and said goodbye. He said he would walk her home, and so they left together. She told me that neither of them spoke during the short walk home, but as they approached the house, he held her hand, pulling her back a little. It was getting dark and she could see the yellow lamplight in the window of our house. She did not resist however and let him kiss her again.

I asked her repeatedly, "why?" He was married and much older than she was. She could not give me a complete answer. All she could say was that he made her feel good and he was kind to her. At home she was expected to cook, wash, look after the children and so on. When she was with him, he treated her like a grown-up.

A few days later, while our father was still away, circumstances took control and she found herself alone with him again. This time, kisses turned to touching and touching turned to sex. She never thought of the consequences, least of all becoming pregnant. All she said was that he was loving, kind, gentle, and she felt like a woman.

Thinking back, I do remember a change in her. She would avoid certain subjects we indulged in, like that of boyfriends, and she even appeared uneasy around our mother. Maybe my mother's instinct told her something was wrong. On two or three occasions, she would ask if my sister was all right and my sister would snap at her, something she had never done before.

But I was the first to know. My period was always a few days before my sister's. Mine came and went and then I realised that hers had not arrived. Sleeping in the same bed together and seeing each other's mood change during the start of menstruation made knowing personal things almost second nature to us. I mentioned to her one night when all the other occupants of the bedroom were fast asleep that her menstruation was late. She looked at me, then burst into tears.

I held her in a sisterly embrace. After a few moments, she signalled for me to follow her outside, not wanting to disturb the little ones. We sat on the small wooden bench that my father had erected by the entrance to the driveway. The night air was cool and sounds of insects filled the air. I gave her a minute to calm down, my arm around her shoulders, then asked her again.

"I think I'm pregnant," was all she could say before she was overcome by tears again. I cried with her for what seemed a long time.

She took a deep breath and between sobs related what had happened. When she finished, we again sat and talked for a while. My father would be due back in a few days, so we decided that it would be best to tell our mother first. Our father would receive the news better from his wife than from his now pregnant daughter. Either way, we knew there would be trouble.

When the little ones were not around, we three sat down and my sister poured out the story. Holding each other's hands while she related the whole story, it was as if I was part of the saga. My mother simply sat and listened, and took the news as if she already knew about it, except for wiping away a small tear from her eye. When the story was done, my mother leaned forward, took my sister in her arms and held her close, stroking her long black hair and whispering in our native dialect, *eka migaganaka agabusan mu yan*, never mind, never mind. For a good ten minutes we sat like that, me holding my sister's hand and she with her head cradled against my mother's chest, her eyes flowing with tears again.

The day my father returned was a day my sister and I were dreading. We were, to say the least, on edge, but my normally submissive mother suddenly changed. She planned ahead and sent us both to see her sister in Tarlac, a neighbourhood to the north of Angeles City, telling us to remain there until we heard from her. She was not unlike a lioness protecting her cubs from the angry male lion. She took charge of the whole situation and until today my sister admires her for that. Not being there, we could only surmise what was happening and it wasn't until some time afterwards that we found out my father's true reactions. Yes, he blamed his daughter, but he blamed his longtime friend twicefold. The father of the child now growing inside my sister's womb had not been told of the pregnancy, not by my sister or my mother. Though my sister and the man had remained in touch until we departed for Tarlac, my mother had sworn us to not say anything. So when my father broke the news to him it must have been a bombshell.

I have to say now that my father showed unusual restraint. He did not storm over to the house and confront the man in front of his family as many others might have done, but rather waited until the next time they met at the midweek *sabong*—the local cockfight. The sabong was an almost all-male affair in the village. It was treated not only as a spectacle and a chance to win some money, but also as a place to socialise and rehash local gossip.

The sabong was built around the cockfighting pit, a hundred yards back from the road. Tall Narra timbers encircled the wooden steps that provided tiered platforms for spectators. A corrugated iron roof gave some relief from the burning midday sun. Men and boys from the neighbouring barrios would descend in droves, some to place bets, others to compete. Prized cocks were first brought into the matching room, a small bamboo hut where the owners and handlers would size up their fighting birds, looking for weight and aggression, as they tried to find a match that would hopefully give their cock an edge.

I had never been inside a sabong, but if you walked past it on fighting days, the noise from within was deafening. I could only guess at the excitement inside but knew that one cock would die and the winning side won money from the death. As Christos placed their bets, the noise would increase in volume, then there would be a sudden hush as the fight began, followed by "oh's" and "ah's", increasing in decibels as the fight progressed. Sometimes the fight lasted for a mere minute, but never more than ten, for if both cocks were still alive after ten minutes, the referee would declare it a draw. But when one cock was killed, an uproar invariably ensued as the winner celebrated and the loser argued for an excuse.

* * *

My father never told us of the man's reaction. He might well have been, for all we know, full of remorse. But they certainly did not come to blows. And even though they remained friends, the closeness of their friendship would never be the same.

A plan had to be made and once again my mother took the lead. The man was told never to talk about the child even to his own wife. Marriage and abortion were not options, so the plan had to include an excuse to keep my sister away from the barrio during her pregnancy—away from the gossip and shame that would inevitably follow, and certainly she must be kept away from the child's father and his family. We announced that my sister was going to Tarlac to help look after my mother's sister, who was generally known to be in poor health.

Unwanted pregnancies had happened before, not only within our community, but all over the country, so there was always a previous case to base the plan on. There were of course the normal adoption agencies operating throughout the Philippines, but that meant more chance of people finding out. My mother and father wanted to avoid this type of gossip so they chose a different route. Through a friend in Manila and without disclosing that it was their daughter, my parents found a couple who wished to adopt a baby. Once my father had accepted the situation and ensured that he and his family would not become the centre of local gossip, he took over what was in essence my mother's plan and put it into action. All my sister was told about the plan was that she should have the baby and it would be adopted, and that she should remain in Tarlac until the whole thing was over.

While I do not think that my sister had considered keeping the child, I do not think she had given thought to how she would feel in giving it up either. The complications in keeping an illegitimate child were obvious to all those close to the situation. People would know the father had to be someone from within the barrio, as my sister had never been away from home. And there was the child's father and his family to consider. When the news eventually came out, which it inevitably would, what would happen then? No—adoption was the only answer.

What I am about to say may seem harsh to my father, considering how well he took the news of his eldest daughter's pregnancy, and the true affection and understanding he showed for my sister's feelings. But once the plan was laid and everything was in place, he turned the situation to his advantage. My mother later told me that the adopting couple had also agreed to pay for the medical expenses, but I have a feeling that my father struck some type of deal where he too got some money. Certainly after the birth he seemed to have considerably more money in his pocket. The quality and quantity of our food for the next few months improved, and he always seemed to be able to go to the sabong with some extra pesos. I don't blame him if he benefited. In my view what he did to protect my sister from public embarrassment was well worth a small reward, and if it meant that my younger brothers and sisters could eat a little better for a few months, even though it was due to this tragedy, it was certainly worth it.

The father of the child managed to find a job in Saudi Arabia. By strange coincidence, it involved driving a truck between the building sites of the many new developments in that country. He left some two months before the birth and was never, as far as I know, told whether the child was a boy or a girl. And he also never knew how my sister suffered during the childbirth.

My sister returned to Tarlac as planned. Her time came and she went into labour, but it soon became apparent that there were going to be complications. Her labour and subsequent birth took almost twenty-four hours and she suffered a lot of pain. I was obviously curious to know everything about it and, when she returned home a few months after the birth, I wasted no time in asking her as soon as the opportunity arose.

The quality of medical services, even in Tarlac, were far behind those in Manila. After some twenty hours in labour, and with the baby in obvious difficulty, the surgeon decided to perform a caesarean. To my amazement, my sister revealed that she was not administered a full anaesthetic and suffered considerable pain during the operation. She told me that at one point she felt God was punishing her with this pain because of her sin with the man. When I saw the scar that was left I could not believe it, literally from her naval down to her *pec-pec*. Months afterwards, the scar remained ugly and red and never seemed to heal properly.

To this day, she still looks at it in the mirror, probably wondering how one silly moment of passion resulted in her being marked for life. She saw the baby—a girl—for only a few moments, but tells me that she can still remember her eyes. The little thing was whisked away as part of the plan. My sister was left in the delivery room with an incompetent surgeon stitching her up and only the memory of the pain mixed with that one moment of joy when she saw her baby's eyes. Needless to say, many tears were shed over the following days and weeks that she remained confined to her bed. In the Philippines, particularly in the provinces, it is a tradition that the mother remain in her bed for a month after the birth. Everything is done for her and for the baby by family members. In my sister's case, there was no longer a baby, but the damage caused by the surgeon forced her to remain in bed for the same length of time. Our mother had conveniently arranged to visit Tarlac around the time of the expected birth, and I know my sister will be forever grateful that she was there to help her through the ordeal.

When she returned home, I noticed she was a different person. Other than asking her about the birth itself I never probed into her feelings. I tried to put myself in her position and imagine what it must feel like to suffer all that pain and yet have nothing at the end of it. There were many nights when I could hear her quiet sobs and feel her body shaking with those silent tears. I would turn over and put my arm around her in an effort to share the pain until she dropped off to sleep. Once or twice when she thought she was alone, I saw her standing before the only mirror we had in the house and looking at the scar, running her finger along it as if reliving the terrible experience, but I never let her see me watching her.

Over the next few months, things began to get back to normal, if they ever could be normal after such an event. My eldest brother knew what had happened, but would never talk about it. The others were too young to understand. They were just pleased to have their big sister back home again. Our youngest sister grew particularly close to my sister, and I wondered if this was a reminder of what might have been if circumstances had been different. Even my father, who was usually distant, seemed to take more interest in us all. It was as if the experience had awakened him to the fact that we, his children, needed him. Some people say that sometimes good can come out of bad experiences. This change in my father was one of those few times.

The peace and calm that had returned to our family was soon to be shattered. Times were hard and money scarce. The truck company that had employed my father had gone out of business. Whether it was bad management, competition from better-funded merchants, or simply bad luck, I don't know. My father did his best to get part-time odd jobs and even worked the fields, but this was not regular work.

I knew that something was going on, but had no real idea exactly what. It was like watching one of those tropical storms brewing before becoming a thunderous rage: the calm, moist, humid air rising up to form the darkening clouds, then the crash of the first lightning bolt and the torrential downpour that turns the dusty, flat barrio roads into instant swamps.

* * *

My father and I sat on the bench outside the house where I had sat with my sister just over a year ago as she told me her bad news. And it was on this bench that my father chose to break the next "storm" to me.

I had noticed his nervousness over the last few days. Whenever worried, especially over money, he had a habit of running his hands through his hair and around his face. He would pinch his nose, moving his head around in a slow circular motion, then lean back, rolling his eyes skyward, his hand still on his face.

"You know we cannot keep you at school any longer," he said. He held my hand as if to comfort me for the shock about to come. "There is no money left." It was as if I could feel the first drops from those storm clouds. "Your mother and I have been talking about this for some time and we think it is best if you go and work abroad."

Fear gripped my throat. I loved my mother and father and my three brothers and three sisters and I would do anything to make their life more comfortable, but I had never been away from the province, except for an overnight trip to Manila airport. I asked "what would I work as?" The answer I received was the final cloud in the sky.

"We thought of you working overseas, maybe in Hong Kong, as a dancer."

I sat stunned. Stories I had heard were flashing through my mind at a hundred miles an hour. I grasped for a thought that I could hold on to, that would make sense of what I was hearing.

"It won't be too bad, you will be okay and make lots of new friends."

"The money is good and you will be able to look after your younger brothers and sisters...."

"You know not finishing school here means it will be impossible to get a well-paid job anywhere in the Philippines."

I could manage only a single question: "When?"

"We will start the paperwork as soon as possible."

He slapped my leg playfully and stood up, kissed the top of my head and said, "Don't worry, you'll be fine, wait and see."

As he walked back to the house, I sat there with a sense of loneliness. In my mind I imagined all my school friends passing by and waving to me. I was in an aeroplane looking out the window. Then I felt someone sit down on the bench next to me and turned to see my sister. She had overheard my father talking to my mother about my reaction.

"Don't worry, it will be all right," she said. She put her head on my shoulder and said no more. We sat motionless with our own thoughts.

2. Dark Clouds

Some days the sky is blue and streaked with white powder. Other days, dark clouds appear. It is strange looking at darkening clouds hanging overhead and feeling no drops. Why would they appear if they meant nothing?

THE NEXT FEW days passed with a quiet apprehension that had overcome everyone in the family. Conversation was restricted to ordinary matters and nothing was said about the future. My eldest sister and I were drawn closer together. We spent much of our time talking about when we were younger and freer—free from her sad memories and free from thoughts about our future. Just as I had shared in her recent pain, she seemed now to want to share in mine.

One day the "promoter" arrived. He sat outside with my father for over an hour, drinking San Miguel beer and talking. I only saw him for a few minutes, when my father called me to bring out some more beer and ice. Even in that brief moment, although I did not look at him, I could feel his eyes looking me up and down as if to determine my potential as a dancer.

He left and nothing happened till the following day, when my father passed me several forms to sign. I recognised one as a passport application. The others I only glanced at, not wishing to show any mistrust in my father, and signed in the blank space. Later we went into town and I had my picture taken for the passport, contract and dance card—all essential to my proposed job in Hong Kong. If I asked about anything, my father would reassure me, saying, "Do not worry about that." Everything seemed to be moving so fast. My mother seemed to distance herself from the arrangements. Whether this indicated her disagreement with the plan or her embarrassment as a mother forced to send her daughter away to take on perhaps distasteful work, I do not know. When the subject did come up, I asked her what would happen if I did not like it in Hong Kong. She told me to ask my father.

My eldest sister was always there to talk to, but the younger ones saw only people visiting me, and me signing forms and having my photograph taken. They were drawn into the activity and my youngest sister pinned one of the spare photographs over her bed. It was not long before other members of the family knew about the plans and, when they visited us, all they wanted to do was to talk about my move to Hong Kong. I was not accustomed to all of this attention, and suppressed any feeling of being a scapegoat for the family, their chance to improve their quality of life at my expense.

I would say that I was going to visit my grandmother, but this was often an excuse to be alone with my thoughts. I would stroll up the dusty road and walk by the rice fields toward her house. Sometimes I would drop in, other times I would simply carry on walking, following the little stream that separated the rice fields from the houses. My thoughts would turn to the dreams that I had had about going to college and becoming a teacher, of getting married and having a family of my own. I enjoyed the solitude away from the conversations, but during the walks I would still feel that grey cloud hanging over my mind.

A week later my father announced that we would be visiting the promotion in Angeles. Located in the southern part of Pampangan Province, Angeles City was some two hours north of Manila by car. Angeles was a long-time trading destination in the northern Philippines but came into prominence when the US military built Clark Air Base there in the 1960s. Even with the closure of the air base in 1991, following the eruption of Mt Pinatubo, many of the American military community and retirees stayed on, and so did some of the bars and infrastructure.

The night before our visit, I spoke to my sister for the first time of my fears. Up until then, I had tried to keep an open mind. I knew that people sometimes exaggerated, and I put many of the bad stories that I heard into this category. I had also heard from others about the good side of Hong Kong and this encouraged me. There was the freedom from the family, new friends and the very experience of going abroad. But that night, my fears returned. I confided in my sister that if I felt like this now, going only 20 miles to Angeles, what would I feel like when it was time to leave for Hong Kong?

* * *

When we arrived in Angeles, my father disappeared with the promotion staff and I was left with some of the other girls in a small dining area. An old, kind-looking lady appeared and placed some food on the table. We all thanked her in unison and started eating. My apprehensions faded as we ate and talked. I was not the only one who had heard horror stories about being a dancer overseas, nor was I the only one who was afraid of leaving home.

Our chatting was interrupted by one of the managers, who told us to go into the dance room. As we walked along one behind the other, like ducks following their mother, I glanced into a room and caught a glimpse of a group of girls dancing to music who seemed to be enjoying themselves. At the end of the corridor we entered the room. I could see all the fathers including mine standing at one end. In front of the mirrored wall were four chairs, three already occupied, and the fourth waiting for the manager escorting us. He beckoned us to stand across the wall facing the chairs. We nervously shuffled into position.

The only lady of the group stood up and addressed us. She was a little on the plump side, much like my mother, but very well dressed, and I noticed a gold ring on each finger. She had a commanding voice and we were all, I am sure, a little frightened. We were to take two steps forward, give our name, age and where we were from, then walk slowly to the end of the line. I was pleased that I had squeezed myself into the middle of the group and so was not first. This was to be my first experience of being on display, something that would be repeated during my training and again in Hong Kong—but there it would be very different. Our little parade completed, we were told to return to the dining room.

Other girls who were obviously well into their training were eating away and the noise from their chatter filled the dining room with a garbled sound. As we approached, they stopped talking and their eyes followed us as we seated ourselves. They did not attempt to talk to us, but returned to their meal and conversation. A few minutes later one of the fathers appeared and called his daughter over. He opened the door for her and followed her out. It was the last time we saw her.

"Too fat," my father explained on the drive home in a small jeepney borrowed from his brother. "That's why we had to go today," he continued. "They're not going to waste time and money on a girl if she is not going to be any good." I felt a little sorry for the girl. She seemed nice.

My mother commented that I appeared to be more cheerful about the "job", as it was now described in conversation. Even in that short meeting designed as the final selection process, I had met two girls in particular who were going to be important friends for me. And already the excitement of some of the group had rubbed off on me. It was the talk of extra freedom, of not having to do the family washing or to look after younger brothers and sisters and, more importantly, of having money to buy things. At home most girls from the age of eight or nine helped with all household chores. Filling the water buckets from the communal pumps, shopping for and preparing the food, washing the clothes or even gathering firewood. All of these were activities that we young girls took for granted. So not having to cook and wash the dishes was, in itself, a minor blessing.

That night, as the others slept, I sat outside with my sister. It was the last time we would spend alone together, just talking, before my departure for Angeles. Two days later, with a few clothes in my bag, I left for Angeles to start my training. As I stood by the door to our bedroom, I could not imagine what my new life would be like. All I could see was my small table in the corner with built-in checkerboard top and the now empty space left on top of my bamboo bed, in a room that had been my home and sanctuary. The loose covers scattered on unmade beds, the clothes strewn around the floor—they were all gone.

* * *

The beds at the promotion centre lined the walls of the dormitory rooms. My father placed my bag on one of the beds and said a short goodbye. I unzipped the bag and placed my few belongings on the shelf next to

21

the bed. Almost as soon as my father left, I had an empty feeling inside me and sat alone on the bed, feeling sorry for myself.

That first feeling of being alone, both physically and emotionally, is hard to describe. I looked around the dormitory. Most of the two rows of beds, each with a simple white sheet and pillow, were empty and seemed to reflect the emptiness in my heart. Searching for a distraction, I looked to the garden outside to watch two brightly coloured birds fighting, as if trying to assume each other's position on the branch of the tree. One of them would launch into the air and circle around, then with wings flapping land back on the branch with a loud screech. The other bird would watch, head cocked on one side, until dislodged by the first bird. I stood there by the window, breathing in the warm scented air and watching this comical spectacle.

The arrival of the other girls, the sight of familiar faces and our zealous chat over lunch helped my homesickness to once again fade. After lunch we were all summoned into one of the practice rooms. We squatted on the floor in front of the lady seated on the only chair in the room. She was to become our "mama" for the duration of our stay. She explained our training schedule and, more importantly, the rules of the house. We were to rise at seven in the morning, wash, change and be in the dining room by eight. Two hours of warm-up exercises and basic dance steps would follow, after which time we would be given a snack— we would later find out that this was a plain corn cracker and a glass of water. This would be followed by our first group dance class and details of what this entailed would be supplied at the time. Lunch and a dance-and-posture class filled the afternoon, after which we would have some time to relax. Those "not up to scratch" could expect additional lessons. The whole process would take around three to four months; this was to allow time for our passports, visas and work papers to be processed and to ensure we were properly trained. At the end of our training we would have to go to Manila and perform a group dance in front of the POEA or Philippine Overseas Employment Agency. If successful, we would receive our "dance card"—the final and, after the passport, the most important document required for Hong Kong. If we did not get this, then it would be back to the promotion for more training.

All of this did not sound too difficult, but the rules of the house were something else. One most important rule which "Mama" emphasised at least three times was "Nobody is allowed out of the complex by herself and never without permission." If we needed something that was not readily available, we had to ask her and she would arrange for it. There was to be no smoking and strictly no food in the dormitories. Any girl found using drugs would be punished and sent home.

"The police," she added, "often come here to check on us, and we do not want any trouble, do we?"

No telephone calls. This seemed a strange rule. No one I knew had a telephone and it must have been the same for the others. If we did have someone to call, it would be almost impossible to do so as the only phone was in a side office and this was either locked or manned all the time. Besides, I don't think any of us girls had ever used a telephone before.

"No visitors without permission and strictly," she paused to look us all in the eye one by one, "strictly no boyfriends." Checking the piece of paper in her hand, she searched for missing points.

"You will be called in the morning, just before seven. It is up to you to get yourselves up for breakfast and off to your class. You will not be reminded."

She folded the paper and tossed it to the floor next to her brown leather bag. "Any girl who is late for her class or lunch or any other activity…" She paused yet again and gave us a stare that we were to see often over the next few months—it said *I mean business*. "Any girl who is late for anything will be punished or fined." She stood up and took a few paces toward us. She did not single out any particular girl but seemed to be looking at us all together.

She concluded, "We are here to help you." She swept her arm along the line of girls. "Waste our time, or think that this is just a game, think again. You're all here to work and I will make sure you do. If you mess around or fall behind, you answer to me."

She paused, then in an almost comical way added, "You can call me Edna." She turned, walked back to the seat, stooped and picked up her handbag. "Right, off you go to Room B. Mr Jemez is waiting to see you."

With that, she opened the door and left.

We sat there looking at each other for a few moments. Then one of the girls said in a sarcastic voice, "Yes, Ate Edna—" We fell about laughing.

* * *

Edna had a commanding presence. Her manicured nails, delicate makeup and well-kept hair inspired confidence. In her youth she must have been attractive. Her skin was still soft but time had drawn lines near her eyes and middle age was thickening her waistline, which even her smock-like dresses could not disguise. In truth, what most defined her character was not what maturity had bestowed but rather what age had taken away. What may once have been a fresh, youthful demeanour was all but gone and compassion had been replaced with detachment and short temper. Perhaps drudgery was to blame. Perhaps the real culprit was not any single bad experience but dreams unfulfilled.

Sheena and Baby were my first two friends at the promotion. We linked arms and marched off to Room B. "She's a bit of an old dragon," said Sheena. We both agreed that, as of now, that was what we would call her privately.

Sheena gave the impression of not being scared of anyone. Tall, long-legged, slim, pretty and confident with an air of dominance, she took control of situations. Her voice seemed to match her height, being a little higher in pitch and squeaky when excited. Baby was more like me and only a few months younger. She was in my opinion by far the best-looking girl in our group. And though she probably knew it herself, she always placed herself behind others. She was named Baby, she told us, because she had a rounded face and was the youngest in her family. She had soft tanned skin and silky hair that flowed across one side of her forehead and down over her shoulders. Her voice was almost the opposite of Sheena's, low and sexy. But when she laughed she achieved a pitch that challenged Sheena's and rang in your ears.

"Come on in girls, don't be shy!" Mr Jemez's voice was discernibly high. That one sentence told us that Arnie, as we were to call him, was clearly not that interested in girls. But it was calming to hear his cheerful voice and see a smiling face, especially after our last twenty minutes or so with the dragon.

"Right, my name is Arnie. I will be your dance teacher, choreographer, friend and anything else you please. Right, before we begin, hands up girls if you have done any dancing before." He looked around expectantly. "Oh, come on now girls. You must have danced at the barrio fiesta, or at a wedding or something?" He smiled at the sight of two or three hands raised. "Good. At least some of you know what we are here to learn."

"Right." I couldn't help noticing that he started every sentence this way. "For those of you who have not danced before, I am going to teach you and when I am finished you will all be great dancers." He paused, smiling again and looked along the line.

"Right."

There he goes again, I thought.

"Let's get some names first." He grabbed a handwritten list and a slightly chewed pencil.

"Who's first?"

As was to happen many times in the future, it was brave Sheena who took the lead. "Sheena Padua, nickname is She-She," she said.

"Good, Sheena," he said, making a tick against her name. "Nicknames are fine by me. Next!" And so it went on until his list was completely marked.

The day drifted by. Edna passed out some forms for us to sign along with the notice of our class schedule. I recognised my father's signature on the form, which basically said that the promotion would cover the cost of our food and lodging and that this would be deducted from the first three months' salary once we reached Hong Kong. Little did we realise that this single piece of paper would have a large impact on our salaries later on. But at the time, with our father's name and signature already in place, it seemed like a very straightforward document.

That night after dinner, Sheena, Baby and I asked Edna if we could sit outside on the steps at the front of the building. It was Sheena's idea so we let her do the talking.

"Just for an hour," said Edna, then added, "I will be out later to check that you're there." She made her point firmly. We nodded and headed for the front door.

"Are you excited about going to Hong Kong?" Sheena began. Baby started to answer. While seeming to listen, I slipped back into my thoughts. So far things did not seem so bad. We had good food. My new friends were fun. We each had a bed to ourselves, a luxury. The work did not seem to be too difficult. In fact, it looked as though it could be exciting. Except for Edna, everybody seemed nice—some a little strange, but generally nice. There were the strict house rules, but they had to keep a close eye on us girls. Our parents would expect it. My mind was already doing a balancing act, weighing my life back home with my expectations of life in Hong Kong, and from what I had seen so far, Hong Kong was winning. Was it the added freedom, my new friends, the thought of having my own bed and money in my purse? I don't know.

When my mind returned to the present, the other two were still chatting away. Baby sat on the step in front of Sheena, who was plaiting her long black hair. I watched, half listening to them and half listening to the annoying roar of the tricycles speeding past the perimeter wall.

I jumped in. "What about going out with the customers?"

The two girls turned around and looked at me. Almost in unison they asked, "Are you still a virgin?"

I nodded.

"No problem," Sheena smiled. "You just have to dance and drink and make as much money as you can."

"They can't force you, you just have to keep saying *no*."

"What about you?" I asked.

Sheena stopped working on Baby's plait and looked up into the partly clouded sky as if she was searching for the perfect answer.

"Well, it would depend."

"On what?"

"Well, I am not a virgin, but I don't have that much experience, so I guess it would depend on the guy." She had obviously thought about this before. "I know that you can earn a lot more money if you go out, but I think I will try and find just one person I like, and then, if I go out, it will just be with him." She went back to the plaiting.

I was to learn that "finding just one person", as Sheena suggested, was the hope of most of the girls who went overseas.

"What about you, Baby?"

"I'm a bit like Sheena. I lost my cherry about six months ago and that was a mistake because I have not seen him since. And I thought he was my boyfriend."

"So you've only done it once?" Sheena asked.

"Three times actually and I am not sure if I want to do it again. I certainly haven't even thought about going out with the customers." She ran her hands over the finished plait and added, "I will wait until I get to Hong Kong and then see how I feel."

"Five minutes, girls, and then inside." True to her word, Edna came to check on us.

"Yes, Ate," we replied, not turning. And as the door clicked shut, Baby whispered, "You old dragon."

* * *

The subject of the customers and Hong Kong would crop up again before we left Angeles City.

"I'm glad we met each other," I said, placing my arm around their shoulders as we stood up.

"So am I," they both replied.

Sheena said, "Let's get to bed. I'm tired and tomorrow we have our first dance class with Arnie." Hands on her hips, she wiggled with an exaggerated walk and effeminate hand movements. "Our lovely instructor," she sighed, in a higher than normal tone.

Giggling, we turned in.

I slept well that night. Sheena and Baby's friendship cast a spell over me. Most of the girls had already formed themselves into smaller groups through which they, like me, could confide, share fears and draw strength from each other. Sheena had already become my strong companion, someone I could trust and who would be there to help me out, almost like a guardian angel. Baby was more of a soulmate, like me in many ways, inwardly worried about what might lie ahead, but outwardly putting on a brave face. It was as if she wanted to be seen by others to be brave like Sheena, but underneath I could see that she too was keeping her fears locked away inside. We both needed Sheena to bolster our courage, but in the end we would both need each other even more. Sheena, indeed, could survive alone; Baby and I would require each other's strength.

Sure enough, our wake-up call arrived. I sat up in bed and looked at the sunlight coming in through the window of the second floor dormitory. *Another hot day ahead*, I thought as I grabbed my towel and hairbrush from the small bamboo bedside locker.

I couldn't help but notice how the facilities at the promotion signalled an improvement in my life. At home the electricity that fed low wattage light bulbs was intermittent and unreliable, yet during my stay in the promotion I never experienced a "brown out" (electricity power cut). The two-ring LPG gas burner that my mother used seemed positively antique compared to the gas oven and hob at the promotion. Even though I was not required to buy or prepare the food, I noticed that instead of buying ingredients on a meal-by-meal basis, as was the case at my home, the promotion had a refrigerator where food could be stored and kept fresh for several days.

The second floor shower room had two toilets, both separated from shower cubicles by a bamboo screen. Halfway up the plain concrete walls was a tap from which cold water would rush when the valve was opened. We ran the water into a small hand-held bucket to pour over ourselves. In the province water had to be pumped from a communal well outside and carried into the house.

Soap and shampoo soon became "shared items" owing to the difficulty of keeping track of them. Outside the dormitory next to the showers was an anteroom. There was a long bench on one side with a row of mirrors hung just above the surface of the bench. After showering, we spread out in a line in front of the mirror to brush our hair and get ready. There was a constant mixture of voices merging into one another, laughter and shouts of *that's my brush, where's my toothpaste* or *give me that* ringing out into the corridor.

I soon learned not to be the last one out of bed. With some forty girls in the promotion at any one time, the place was a zoo first thing in the morning, and queuing up for the toilet or shower meant being late for breakfast. It was not long before the three of us worked out a routine. One would grab the toilet, the other the shower, and we would rotate the use of them between us. Several of the other girls had the same idea, so each morning became a constant battle among the various groups.

Those who made it through the early bedlam first enjoyed the best selection of food, yet another good reason for not lazing in bed till the last moment. By now we were mingling with the other girls at the promotion, though we all tended to keep ourselves to our own training groups. During mealtimes the constant chatter of dialects melded together. Never had I heard so many different dialects at once. Of course, if a girl was talking in Pampangan, my local dialect, I would instinctively turn to see if I recognised her.

Breakfast consisted of a small bowl of rice, a piece of dried fish and perhaps a small selection of green vegetables. Now that we were well and truly part of the whole group, our food became boring and less plentiful. This was totally unlike our sumptuous welcoming meal which consisted of grilled Bangus (a tasty white-flesh fish), Sinigang na Hipon (a mixed vegetable dish consisting of swamp cabbage, sitao, ginger, long green chillies, onions and thin green beans), Chicken Adobo (a familiar dish stewed in vinegar and garlic) and, of course, plain rice.

At home, it was not uncommon to eat rice at virtually every meal. For large families, food was precious and variety was not as important as quantity. On one occasion I heard a girl ask one of the mamas if she could have some extra. The reply was short and sharp to the effect that "It's more than you would get at home and we don't send fat girls to Hong Kong." During my stay I never saw a plate returned to the kitchen with food left on it.

* * *

The days passed quickly. We did our dance routines, practised the splits, and tried to keep busy. We three spent a lot of our time together, whether talking in the garden, flipping through old magazines or listening to music on the radio. We got to know each other very well, our childhood days, school—what there was of it—and our dreams for the future. In fact we must have talked about every subject under the sun, including sex and customers again and again. The strange thing to me was that I could now talk about customers without the fear that used to grip me. The real customers were still a long way away, and Sheena and Baby did not seem concerned, so why should I worry? Without realising it, I was absorbing some of Sheena's confidence and Baby's poise. The more time I spent with them, the better I felt.

"Just drink and dance," Sheena often said. "It's as simple as that. Remember, you are the one who is in control."

The two of them often made the joke that I must be saving myself for my future husband and how they hoped he would appreciate it.

Like most of the other girls, I enjoyed Arnie's company and felt safe with him, even when he touched us, holding our waist as we twisted around or lifting a leg as we kept our balance. His touch never seemed to have a physical meaning. Unlike our manager, Len's. I found out that Len was related to the owner of the promotion. He was about 5 feet 5 inches, with a protruding stomach that stretched the black leather Satchi belt around his waist. He wore flashy clothes, and maybe he thought that these clothes, the gold neck chain, and the shiny watch would help him look younger. His hair had flecks of grey, which sometimes would appear to be glossy and black, indicating that he had the money to dye his hair. His ensemble of clothes, jewellery, hair dye and the imported cigarettes that seemed to be forever burning between his fingers made him look out of place.

On a few occasions, he would visit the dance class and watch us. When Arnie split us into smaller groups, which he often did, Len would make a point of talking to the girls who were not dancing. The conversation was normally polite—*How are you doing? Are you enjoying it?* and so on. But on more than one occasion Len would put his arm around a girl and give her a squeeze.

He did it to me once and whispered, "You're very beautiful, Mary. Arnie might be able to teach you to dance, but I could teach you to dance in bed." Then he added, "Don't worry. I'll make it worth your while."

I pulled away, a cold shiver running down my back. He smiled in his superior way and moved over to another girl, looking back to see if I was watching him while he gave her a cuddle. This was the first time anyone had ever talked that way to me. The experience was a shock and immediately brought back to mind all those fears of the "customer".

That night, after dinner, I pulled Sheena to one side and told her to go outside. She asked Edna for permission and told Baby to meet us.

"You seem upset," Sheena said, placing her arm around me as we sat down on the concrete step that was becoming almost as familiar as the bench outside my father's house.

"You've been so quiet all afternoon, what's wrong?"

I started relating the incident about Len, telling of my fears. Sheena stopped me before I was finished.

"Don't you worry about Len. He won't do anything to you." She squeezed my shoulder. "He's just a dirty old letch and tries it on with all the girls. He has already tried it on with me and Baby and most of the other girls as well."

"I told him," Baby interrupted, "that his *titi* would never be big enough to satisfy me and that he should try it with Edna instead."

We burst into laughter as Sheena went on about the size of Len's manhood. Without these two I don't think I would even have made it through the training, let alone to Hong Kong. Whenever something came up Sheena and, to a lesser extent, Baby were always there to sort me out. In this case though, my instinct about Len was to be proved right. It would involve a girl we had come to know as Mika.

Mika came from a little village a few miles north of Zambales. From what we heard, she was one of nine children and her family was very poor. Even my family was better off. Her only asset was her beauty and she certainly was attractive—young, slim, shy and with an innocence you could see in her eyes. Even though English is the second language taught in Philippine schools, her English was nonexistent, a sign that there was no money available for her to complete her basic schooling. The ever-watchful Edna had noticed this. Hong Kong, she told us, was a "very international place" with many different languages spoken, and we would be expected to speak English as well as know greetings in Chinese, Japanese and Korean. At the very least, because there were so many tourists, expatriate workers and visiting naval vessels, we were expected to be able to converse in basic English. Later, in Hong Kong, I found that this language skill was one of the reasons why the bar owners preferred Filipinas to Thai girls; we were both as a race attractive but our English was generally better. Language was definitely going to be a problem for Mika. Edna told her that if she did not learn English she would have to leave the promotion. None of us were that good in English ourselves, and with the short amount of free time in the evening we had no opportunity to teach her. So Len stepped in and offered his services. I suspect to this day that Edna had arranged the whole thing. Twice a week after dinner Mika would receive English lessons from Len.

When the whole sordid story came out, I felt physically sick. Len did indeed improve Mika's English over the next three or four months, but he also took her virginity and made her pregnant. In fact, before Mika was to travel to Hong Kong, she had had two abortions. One was caused by Len and the other by a high-ranking police officer who was a good friend of Len's and a protector of the promotion.

As Mika told us later in Hong Kong, "There was nothing I could do about it." She was told that Len was not charging her extra for the English lessons and was in fact sending money back to Mika's family to help them. If she did not go along with what Len wanted, including entertaining his friends, then she would be out of the promotion. That would mean no possibility of going to Hong Kong to earn much-needed money for her family and a hefty bill to settle with the promotion for the costs incurred to date for her training.

"Why didn't you say anything about what was going on?" we quizzed her. She was frightened of Len and of her father and had been told by Len not to say anything to the other girls. So she just kept quiet and pushed her feelings deep inside.

"What about the abortions?" one of us asked.

"You remember when I missed class because I had a fever? That was the excuse they used when they took me to the clinic."

* * *

My father visited me one day. Edna had given him permission, and though I still had that little feeling of him being to blame for all this, it was good to see him. He told me that everyone was fine but they missed me. Hearing him talk about my younger sisters made me realise I missed them too. I had been so wrapped up in the training and with my new friends, I just had not thought much about them. The one treat during his visit was that Edna allowed him to take me out for lunch. It was nice to see him for the few hours he stayed but it was even nicer to get out from the complex for a while.

* * *

Arnie always seemed to be happy and made us laugh. He enjoyed showing off when we had made a mistake in a dance routine.

"When you turn around, do it like this," he would say, accentuating the move and finishing perfectly. "Right, now try it again and keep your head up. Don't look at your feet."

The only time in my whole training when I became annoyed with Arnie was during a special stretching exercise that Edna insisted we all do. Edna had joined the group during one of the morning sessions, probably to see how we were getting on. But during a short break she had us all line up again. Walking along the row, she prodded our stomachs, mumbling to herself. None of us girls could be described as fat—that had been taken care of during the first visit to the promotion. What was she up too? After her second time along the line she instructed Arnie to give us all stretching exercises. This turned out to be another promotion ploy to apply pressure, and another excuse to introduce the "fines" that Edna had warned us about.

"Don't worry about not having money for the fines," Edna said as she stepped back in front of the line. "They will be added to your promotion bill." She told Arnie to start with the exercises after dinner, then left the room still mumbling to herself about not sending fat girls to Hong Kong.

The exercise was for us girls to lie on our back with hands clasped behind our head, and raise our legs a foot or so off the floor and hold the position, keeping our feet together. It did not sound difficult, yet doing it was excruciating. There was an old clock in the room with a small hand that had long stopped, but the second hand still worked. We would all be grunting and groaning, watching the hand complete a full circle. Those whose feet touched the floor during this minute were added to the "fine list" and had to do it again. It was torture. What this had to do with dancing I will never know, but it was to become a twice-a-week routine. Once again, the promotion was demonstrating their complete control, and an opportunity to chip away at our self-confidence.

3. Green Seas

Rice can grow in the wild, but to be grown in substantial quantities it must be cultivated. For nearly three months the rice seed lives below the water's surface, absorbing moisture and nutrients from the soil. Rows are systematically planted and irrigation is controlled. Once the rice seeds have matured fields are drained to expose the seedlings to the sun's rays. The "green seas" soon turn brown and the rice stalks are ready to be cut, harvested and processed.

WE HAD BEEN practising for almost four months when Arnie announced that we would be going before the Philippine Overseas Employment Agency in Manila in two weeks' time. His announcement sent a shock wave through the group—we were almost there! We jumped up and down and hugged each other, forcing Arnie to shout to calm us down. I do not really know whether we were excited because we saw an end to our training, that we might soon be on our way to Hong Kong or because we had seen the excitement the "POEA dance" had generated in the other groups of girls.

"What it means," Arnie forcefully told us, "is a lot more hard work." He explained that our dance sequences were still not smooth. Several parts of the POEA dance would require individual movements without disrupting the group as a whole. "Right!" he said, pointing his head in all directions.

Toward the end of a very hard lesson Edna popped her head around the corner of the door. "After lunch I want you all to go to the storeroom to get your costumes." This announcement was followed by another noisy buzz. The costumes were for the POEA dance routine. I had only seen glimpses of them from photos hanging in the promotion office. Up until now we had danced and exercised in cutoff jeans, shorts, tee shirts or on very hot days in just shorts and a bra.

It is amazing how the costumes could generate such excitement among us girls. We all came from poor families and had never had the chance to wear nice clothes, so the thought of wearing beautiful dresses thrilled us. We were all used to hand-me-down clothes; even my first Holy Communion dress had been used by my elder sister and before that by others in our extended family. It would not be until I got to Hong Kong that I would buy my first new piece of clothing. Even the bra and panties that I had came from my sister. At home we would simply share them: we were more or less the same size so it seemed natural. The conversation over lunch inevitably turned to the subject of costumes, with all of the girls speculating what they would be like. Sheena was her normal outrageous self, saying she wanted something bright, red and very flashy. Normally we would dawdle over lunch in an effort to shorten our afternoon dance lessons, but today everybody raced through the meal, eager to get to the costumes.

The storeroom was a giant wardrobe with rails at one end from which dozens of dresses hung and mirrors and wooden benches lining the other walls. The room had a musty smell, indicating that it was not used often. Edna was already there with another of the mamas, Winnie, who was busy lifting the plastic covers from the hanging rails. As she pulled at the covers dust rose into the air and danced in the rays of sunlight streaming through the windows.

"Okay, girls, take your clothes off and place them on the benches."

We stripped down to bras and panties. With her assistant Winnie, Edna picked out some of the dresses and placed them on a small table. They were all pink and low-backed, had spaghetti shoulder straps and fell to just above the knees. Embroidered belts held the waist with a large pink bow tied at the back.

"Sheena, you're tall, try this one," she said, holding up one of the dresses, "and Annie, try this one." Sheena did not get her bright red dress but she smiled as she held her substitute dress against herself, observing it in the mirror.

The door opened and in walked Arnie, followed by Len. I moved to cover myself as Edna called out my name. Clutching the dress in my arms, I shuffled to the corner and slipped the dress over my head.

We stood there like a row of sweetcorn, straight and motionless. Edna walked up and down the line, followed by Arnie. Edna would pull at the waist or around the bust. Arnie would agree that this was too tight, that was too loose. The most embarrassing thing was making changes if Edna didn't think the dress fit. In my case, I had to change twice. And each time I saw Len's eyes upon me, looking me up and down with that smart grin on his face. It was even more nerve-wracking than his first pass at me.

After another week of practice we were ready. We had been told that all of our passports and papers were in place and we only needed the "dance card". That we knew meant dancing to the satisfaction of the POEA judges.

The night before we left for Manila we took up our usual place on the steps. Sitting there, as we had done so many times before, I could hear the sound of the familiar tricycles and jeepneys as they passed by on the road outside. Tomorrow I would start my journey and this thought caused me to wonder where these vehicles were taking their passengers. Buses were for the longer distances between cities and provinces, whereas jeepneys covered the shorter distances within the city and its surrounding areas. Owners purchased a route licence, then sped along the prescribed route, picking up and dropping off passengers. There were no timetables or designated stops: they ran their route and passengers waved them down. The funny thing was that each owner would completely customise the jeepney himself, turning his vehicle into a flashy, open-air "workhorse". You could always find something distinctive about each vehicle, whether it was in the name of the jeepney, its mosaic paint job, metal fenders, tyres, mirrors, ornaments, insignia, flags, flashing lights or even the driver's music selection.

The sounds of jeepneys, mixed with the screams of tricycles, blotted out the hiss and clicking of night insects, which provided a quiet backdrop in between passing vehicles. And there we were—Sheena with arms around our shoulders, Baby and me crouched forward, chins on hands. Without saying a word, we stood up, turned and headed inside.

* * *

We set off for Manila at the crack of dawn to avoid the traffic jam, but this was not to be. A truck had overturned just past Santa Rita and the two lanes were reduced to one. By the time we got to the Balintawak tollgate at the end of the highway the queue was at least four miles long. Edna, who was seated in front, was in a nasty mood. The heat and exhaust smells that flowed into the open jeepney were getting to her. She constantly changed the angle of the small electric fan blowing air across the front seat and fanned herself furiously with an old road map while cursing the traffic. The rest of us in the back sweated it out on sticky plastic-covered seats.

We arrived hot, tired and exhausted. Despite the discomfort, I had enjoyed the journey. I had been to Manila only once before when my father had taken me along to pick someone up from the airport. We travelled there and back at night, so I had never seen Manila in daylight. The traffic was amazing. The sheer number of buses, jeepneys and cars, and the noise from their horns.

Edna wasted no time finding herself a chair in front of the office fan. She called for her assistant Meli to show us to the dormitory. As we followed Meli up the stairs, I noticed how she walked in seesaw fashion. She was obviously from the lower classes, her dark, pitted skin telling the story of a very deprived childhood. The ugly brown marks left on her arms and legs by insect bites indicated that she had probably spent much of her life living under the stars. Her thin, somewhat bent body told that food had been in short supply. Her thick black hair bunched up and poking out from under the white scarf would soon be long enough to cut and sell to the wig merchant. For Meli this would be a bonus of maybe fifty pesos. She looked to be in her mid-thirties, but I later learned that she was only twenty-three.

After we dumped our bags on the beds and kicked off our shoes, Meli asked us to follow her to the dining area. It was a small indoor courtyard. Plants and small trees in tubs lined the walls, and the terracotta floor tiles and white tables and chairs scattered about complemented the green perimeter.

We were all extremely hungry and wasted no time indulging ourselves when the food arrived from the kitchen. During lunch Edna came in and told us that she had to visit some people in Makati and would not be back till late.

"Enjoy your rest," she said. "Tomorrow's a long day."

Morning came and, as anticipated, it was a hot, sticky day. We piled once more into the back of the jeepney, dresses and shoes clasped on our laps. The journey was short, a mile or so further up Roxas Boulevard, but by the time we reached the POEA office our hair was matted and our tee shirts streaked with sweat. Edna signed us in at the guard desk and led us to the changing rooms.

Not more than a half-hour later, we found ourselves on stage in front of the examiners. There were other groups of girls standing around the side of the room. We were understandably nervous and Edna was standing there like a mother duck watching her offspring take to the water for the first time. Finally the music clicked and sounds of familiar beats brought the speakers to life. We let our instincts and training take over. It all happened so fast—the steps, turns, kicks, jumps and spins. No sooner had the music started did it die, and our three-minute routine was over. As the music faded, I knew we must have made a few mistakes, but we remembered to smile at the judges, just as Edna had told us to do.

We had been told that if the judges found us proficient they would raise their thumbs. I had not studied much history, other than the history of the Philippines, but was told that when Roman gladiators fought in ancient times, the Emperor would decide if the loser lived or died with the pointing of his thumb up or down.

The judges—three men and three women—huddled together while we tried to catch our breath and relax. None of us moved or even looked at each other, our eyes were fixed on the judges. Then came the verdict. Thumbs went into the air—we had passed! The commotion on the stage was the release of all our energies, feelings and emotions at the same time. We went around kissing and hugging each other with screams of "we did it, we did it". Sheena gave me a big hug and said in a loud voice,

"Look out Hong Kong, here we come!" Edna congratulated us when we got back to the changing room and Arnie, in a rare moment, let himself go and gave us all a kiss. Sheena grabbed him as he approached her, put her arms around him and gave him a full kiss on the lips. Arnie was stunned and staggered back when Sheena released him. Before he could say anything, she said, "Don't get carried away, Arnie, or I will tell your boyfriend." It was the first time anyone had referred to his sexual preference in front of him. He took it well and smacked Sheena playfully on the backside. We laughed until some of us had tears running down our faces. Edna soon returned to her normal self and told us to quiet down. But looking around at the girls slipping out of their dresses and back into the jeans and tee shirts, you could see the elation and smiles. The smiles all said the same thing—soon we would be away from Edna, away from the promotion and heading to Hong Kong. Even though there were still apprehensive thoughts about what might or might not face us, the sheer joy of having passed was all we wanted to feel for the moment.

On the journey back nobody stopped talking. As we followed the Northern Luzon Expressway back up to Angeles, the jumbled houses and industrial complexes of Manila slowly gave way to palm trees and green, rectangular rice paddies interspaced with patches of brown unseeded ground. As we crossed over the causeway that links Bulacan and Pampanga, I felt a sense of calmness as my eyes searched out familiar terrain. When we arrived, the girls still in the promotion shared in our joy as we had done with other groups before us.

That night, when we took up our places on the steps, we knew it would not be long before we left the promotion for good. Edna had told us on our last night in Manila that in a few days, once the promotion had made our travel arrangements, we would receive our "dance card". We sat there in silence. I looked up at the stars. For once there was a cool breeze and it played a melody with the leaves of the trees. I could almost hear whispering, as if the trees were saying their goodbyes to us.

For the next few days, with little to do, we bombarded Edna with questions: *Would we all work in the same bars? How much would we be paid? Where would we stay? What happens when we get there?* She said little other than that she would do her best to send us all at the same time. As far as salary went, it depended on the hours—the local Hong Kong manager would tell us. We refrained from asking her again because it was obvious that she either would not tell us or did not know. The three of us did, however, pray every night that we would not be separated.

A few days later the news came. Ten of the sixteen girls were to fly to Hong Kong in one week. Edna called us in and was holding a piece of paper in her hand. Still standing in anticipation, we waited for a name to be called before following it up with a rush of congratulations. We waited for the last three names. "Sheena, Baby and Mary." We fell into a joint cuddle and squeezed each other.

"As for the rest of you, it will be about two more weeks, then we will have dates for you."

She folded the paper and left. I could see some disappointment in the faces of those not selected, including Mika's.

"Don't worry," said Sheena, "we will be there waiting for you." We left the room together and I am sure we all said a little prayer of thanks to the Lord at the same time. As we walked past one of the offices, we heard Edna calling us in. We went in and stood in front of her.

"You know, girls," she paused, "it was me that got you all on the same allocation." She gave us a rare smile. "Yes, originally you were to be split up, but I convinced them to keep you all together, knowing how close you all are."

We thanked her, and this time we really meant it.

"So the old dragon is human after all," said Sheena, as we walked back to the dining area.

The next day we were given our papers. This was the first time I had even seen my passport. I held this small document in my hand, a document that would have such a big impact on my life. It was dark blue, embossed with the Philippine coat of arms in gold. Turning the page, I saw the soft textured paper inside punched through with the number of the passport on each page. Then I saw my photo. It was as if I was frozen in time. There I was in black and white, looking younger. My hair was tied back and my smile was forced. There was my name, my date of birth. All I had to do now was sign it and this would be me.

"Do not lose any of these documents or you will not be allowed entry into Hong Kong," Edna lectured, for what was to be the last time. "Tomorrow you will all go home. Don't worry, your parents have been told and are expecting you."

"Next Wednesday," she continued, "you will all return here, before four o'clock in the afternoon. Thursday you go to Manila and your flight to Hong Kong is Friday. You will get your airline tickets when you reach Manila, so make sure you bring all your clothes, and don't forget your documents."

* * *

That was to be the last we would see of Edna, though I would bump into her a few years later. She had done her job, got us through and kept us straight. The girls as a group thanked her politely for all her help. She simply said, "Don't let me down." That night the girls who were to remain hid their disappointment and joined in with our going-away party.

"We'll celebrate with champagne when you all join us in Hong Kong," Sheena said, as she proposed a toast with cups of orange juice.

Back in the dormitory we were all busy packing our few possessions. You could hear cheerfulness mixed with laughter as we took turns making fun of our passport pictures. One strange thing about the photographs was how all of us with long hair had to have it pinned back off our foreheads with a hairband. It was, we were told, a government regulation. For most of us this was unnatural and made for interesting study.

It was a nice feeling to be outside again, with no house rules to follow and no Edna watching our every move. Standing at the bus stop it occurred to me how cut off from the world I had been during my stay in the promotion. I wondered how a novice going into a convent must feel when the door to the outside world closed behind her, and she knew she would not step back out for at least three years. It was good to be back in the world. Baby waved as the bus pulled away, and I sank back against the seat, staring out at the shops, houses and people going about their daily lives.

Sitting there on the wooden seat as the bus bumped its way along, staring out at the now familiar scene, brought back memories of my childhood. How excited I got when my parents took me to Angeles City or Guagua to go shopping, usually for an item or two that couldn't be found in our village. I loved going on the bus. I would sit on my father's lap, my head hanging out of the window, watching the world go by.

As I stared out across the flat landscape, I could see the tall water tower of BASA airbase in the distance. The yellow and black chequered top made it a distinctive landmark for the trainee pilots and all who lived in this area. I daydreamed about the promotion and my two friends. Smiling to myself, I recalled our adventure in Manila on the afternoon before our POEA dance when we had been allowed to go on a brief sightseeing outing and, as usual, Sheena took control.

* * *

"Where are we going?" I asked.

"Luneta Park," said Sheena. "There's a statue of Rizal there."

"It can't be too far from here," she continued. "I know it is on Roxas Boulevard, and I saw that road when we were arriving."

We crossed Roxas Boulevard, a busy, noisy road, and stood there looking out over Manila Bay. I could smell and taste the salt in the air as the waves crashed up against the sea wall. The sea breeze was cool and refreshing. I watched the boats anchored out in the bay rise and fall with the waves.

"Hong Kong is over there," said Sheena, pointing at the horizon.

"How do you know?" asked Baby.

"Well, it's out there somewhere. I'm going to see it soon."

Running along the tree-lined pathway, Baby and I chased her. I had not enjoyed myself for so long. This is what I hoped life in Hong Kong would be like.

We continued our walk arm-in-arm along the Boulevard, looking at all the new sights around us. Sure enough we found the park and the statue of Jose Rizal. Jose Rizal was a hero executed by the Spanish for standing up for the Filipino people against their rule. His statue was mounted on a small pyramid of white stone. I had learned about him at school and knew he was not a tall man, yet standing there in front of me, he appeared enormous. Sitting below him were his guards, looking up toward him. He truly was a national hero. I stood there and stared at the column that towered skyward. I was standing on the very ground of his execution. For once my school history lessons meant something.

The gardens around his memorial were striking. I couldn't remember if any public area in the Philippines was truly beautiful, but to me this was an exception. Tidy flower beds were bursting with scarlet lobelia, laid out in neat squares and surrounded by well manicured lawns.

"I wish I had a camera," said Baby.

"I am going to buy one with my first salary in Hong Kong," Sheena said in a very decided voice, adding that electronic products were supposed to be much cheaper there.

We made our way back, taking time to walk through Luneta Park. There were so many people around. Families having a picnic, children running around in play and of course couples in love, sitting under the trees and finding time to be alone with each other.

* * *

The jolt of the bus hitting the uneven road brought me back from my daydream. Startled, I stared out of the window to get my bearings. I was nearly home.

The excitement at seeing my family continued to build. I stepped off the bus near my old school and crouched into a waiting tricycle for the short journey home down the dusty road. Tricycles are one of the cheapest and most common forms of transport in the local areas and hundreds of boys work through the day and night carrying people, sacks of rice, blocks of ice, chickens—in fact almost anything the passenger wants to transport. As long as they can strap the article onto the trike, they make the journey.

As the sound of the engine was heard in our driveway, all the children came out, throwing themselves around me. I have to admit that I was tearful for the sheer joy of seeing them and being back home. I greeted my parents in the traditional and respectful way, taking their hand in mine and touching it against my forehead, then my mother hugged me. I felt at home once again.

My elder sister was out shopping at the local market. Even with the little money they had, my mother had decided on a family celebration. This meant more and better quality food and perhaps a bottle of Coke. We sat and talked about the last few months. My mother told me I looked thin and wondered if they had fed me. I passed it off as too much work, but she kept squeezing my arm and feeling my stomach.

Within a matter of minutes my relatives had heard of my return and were popping in. My mother would point to my weight loss, insisting that they too squeeze my arm. My brothers and sisters were still hanging around me and getting in the way of conversation, so my father told them to go out to play. When my sister returned I helped her take the food into the kitchen. There, we hugged and looked at each other. Then we said *Are you all right?* at the very same time and burst into laughter.

It was not long before we had caught up on all the gossip. We Filipinos love to gossip and have a wonderful gift of being able to listen and talk at the same time. I told her about Sheena and Baby and how we had become good friends. She laughed over Arnie, how funny he was, and over Edna and her rules. By the end of our conversation she too was referring to Edna as the dragon.

My mother came out and cuddled me again, saying how good it was to see me home again and how she was going to miss me when I went to Hong Kong. I had to shut her up before I burst into tears. I had pushed thoughts of Hong Kong away to the back of my mind and wanted to enjoy my last few days at home with my family.

The meal was as good as any I had eaten, heightened by a few dishes I hadn't seen in a while. I had forgotten how good a cook my mother was. She was determined for me to put back the weight I had lost, twice placing more rice and chicken on my plate. I did my best but could not finish it, leaving my mother to say that she feared for me in Hong Kong as she knew I would skip meals. My little sister, never one to miss an opportunity, asked if she could have the chicken leg that was sitting on the side of my plate.

When my elder sister got up and started to clear the table I tried to help but my mother ordered me to stay. "You take a rest, you deserve it," she said, placing her hand on my shoulder.

We all talked well into the night. My father talked about looking after myself in Hong Kong and my mother, about eating properly. My sister told me I must write every week and send some photographs back. I felt strangely grown-up. Here I was, not the eldest, and setting out on an adventure. Having survived the strictness of the promotion and the ordeal of the dance exam, I felt that with Sheena and Baby's help I could survive anything. Yes, I could even say that I was looking forward to it. I had left my family to go to Angeles, shy and nervous, full of fears and apprehension, and I had returned with a new confidence. I was no longer the little schoolgirl. I had a confidence that was never there before.

I was the first person from my family and one of only a few persons from my extended family to ever visit a different country. All this attention did make me feel special, almost like a celebrity. I handled it in the same way as Sheena would have done. I told them everything would be fine, and though it would be hard work, I was looking forward to it. My confidence reassured my mother.

Tiredness eventually took over and we retired to bed. I had got used to having the whole bed to myself, but when I turned over and my sister placed her arm around me, it felt good and I soon dropped off to sleep.

I had just three days left before I had to return to the promotion and I was determined to make the most of them. I visited what seemed like everybody I had ever known—my old schoolfriends, relatives and especially my grandmother. She had the warmth of a fire inside her and no matter how anyone felt she would always make them feel even better. Everyone I spoke to expected me to write and send pictures.

My shopping list grew and I had not even left yet. I had so many wishes of "good luck" even from people I did not really know.

* * *

The last night arrived and sadness crept in to the point where my younger sisters were pleading with me not to go and my mother became a little withdrawn. My eldest sister was there, keeping me cheerful. Packing my things took all of five minutes. A spare pair of jeans, two pairs of shorts, three tee shirts, one skirt, a few bits of underwear, hairbrush, toothbrush, and most importantly my laminated photograph of the family taken last Christmas. While I was packing with my sister, my mother appeared with a small parcel in her hand and held it out for me. Inside was a nightdress, white with little pink flowers around the neck. I looked up at her. She already had her handkerchief at her eyes.

"Make sure you wear this, it can get cold in Hong Kong."

The tears started and the three of us ended in a huddle, with more tears flowing than there were handkerchiefs to dry them.

Somehow we pulled ourselves together and in between the sobs and sniffing she said, "Come, let's sit down and have some dinner."

I forced myself to eat. There was a new silence around the table, except for the noise of our spoons against the plates. Even the children seemed to sense what was happening. For once they sat and ate their food in silence, without arguments.

I made a point of putting the little ones to bed that night while my mother and sister cleared the table. They were full of innocent questions: *Why are you going to Hong Kong? What are you going to do there? When will you come back?* I answered them all in a roundabout way and told them to be good for mummy and daddy while I was away. I told them that when I came back I would have a special present for each of them. The questions slowly stopped as fatigue set in. I gave them all a kiss and returned to the others.

My mother said she was going to bed early. I think it was because she knew if she stayed up she would cry again, so I went outside to the bench with my sister. We sat there holding hands and looking up at the stars. Our conversation was a mixture of remembrances and dreams for the future. Without desiring it, I had gained a new sense of dominance over my sister. Although she was eldest, her personality had not developed and she remained the quiet and reserved one of the family. My experiences had made me more mature. She now expected me to take the lead in conversation and actions.

The next day saw a constant stream of visitors saying goodbye and wishing me luck, and a constant stream of tears from my mother and me. My father had arranged for his brother to take me back to Angeles City. I had a light lunch, grabbed my bag and, with my handkerchief grasped tightly, gave a final hug and kiss to my family. I left the house and walked straight into the waiting jeepney. I looked back only once and could see my mother peering out from behind the window curtain. Tears took over and would not cease for a few miles. My uncle, bless him, did his best to cheer me up, but I just stared out at the passing scenery and cried.

4. Baby Butterfly

Fly, fly, fly, Oh! Baby Butterfly,

Your time has come,
Your transition now done,

So spread your wings and
take to the sky,

Fly, fly, fly, my Baby Butterfly

I WAS ONE of the first back at the promotion. As we would be there only one night, I did not worry about unpacking my small bag, which contained all that I owned in the world. Dumping my bag on the bed, I went down to wait on the steps for the others. It brought back memories of the day my father drove me here to start my training. This time, oddly, there was no sadness. I looked for the two birds that had helped me forget my homesickness, but they were gone. Sheena bounded into the yard first, bag slung over her shoulder with the confidence that was her trademark. Like me, Baby strolled in, handkerchief still in hand.

The remainder of the afternoon and evening were filled with saying our goodbyes. Arnie was busy with a new group of girls so we stood by the door and watched. It was hard to believe that a few months ago I was going through the same regimen. Arnie came over and gave us all a hug then returned to his lesson. Edna couldn't be found. We spent our last night on our steps talking about our future. None of us had flown before and we spoke mostly about that. I breathed in the warm night air slowly as if my senses wanted to store it away. As I closed my eyes that night I couldn't help feeling a little sad to be leaving.

The early morning jeepney ride was uneventful and we soon arrived at the Manila promotion. Len met us there to give us our plane tickets and airport departure tax money, which he said would be added to our bill. We were to be met by one of the Hong Kong managers and taken to our new apartment and given further instructions. He made cryptic remarks about how he would miss us all and that we should behave ourselves. Then he insisted on kissing us all on the cheek, doing his best meanwhile to squeeze various parts of our bodies. Resisting, I saw that smug little smile that seemed forever fixed on his face. I was glad to get out of the office and away from him for good.

We must have checked the details of our tickets and passports two dozen times before packing them securely in our handbags. With time to spare and no supervision, we considered sneaking out to explore Manila. How exciting it sounded, but the last thing we wanted was trouble, now that we had come this far.

The next day arrived and soon enough we were climbing into the jeepney again, bags on our laps and hope in our hearts. None of us said much on the way to the airport, but we all took our last look at Manila as we sped along Roxas Boulevard, saying our own goodbyes to the Philippines.

The airport was a noisy jumble of people with baggage rushing in different directions. Airport police were directing the human traffic, signalling for people to move inside and constantly blowing their whistles. The inevitable result was a crush of people dragging cases, all trying to enter the departure area at the same time. The security guard at the door checking tickets and passports was creating a bottleneck of his own. We finally squeezed through and Sheena yelled at us to follow her as she pushed through another crowd and headed toward the check-in desk of Philippine Airlines.

Where could all these people be going? I could see businessmen in suits waiting in the line designated First Class. Then there were those in jeans and tee shirts carrying golf bags and doing a good job of knocking people out of their way. Others whom I can only describe as African, dressed in colourful outfits, huddled together pointing this way and that, trying to get someone to tell them where they should queue up. Then there were us, in a line clasping our papers, nervous as hell and trying to act normal, yet not knowing what normal meant.

"Gate number eight, boarding at 14:30." The nice, smartly dressed lady handed back our passports and papers. Heading for immigration, we showed our papers for the third time to the guard at the entrance, queued up to pay the departure tax, then joined one of the long lines in front of the immigration counters.

We chatted away with a nervous delight that was difficult to hide.

"52J, K, and 51H." Sheena said, reading the seat numbers on the boarding cards, adding in disappointment, "That means we are not seated all together."

We were on our way at last, and even the hassle of showing papers and passports, queuing up and getting bumped by strangers in a hurry— none of this could take away the excitement running through our bodies. We shuffled along, getting closer and closer. Sheena was her normal self, joking about some of the other people in the queue. One rather large man, who was perspiring and constantly mopping his brow, was having difficulty keeping his trousers up as he pushed his bag along in front of him with his foot and struggled to hold his carry-on bag in one hand and his papers in the other. His well-rounded stomach forced his trousers down as he wobbled along. Sheena said he would require two seats. Each time he stopped he would put down his carry-on, hitch up his trousers, and tighten the belt, then mop his brow in time to move forward a few more feet before repeating the whole process. The amusement of watching others helped pass the time till we reached the front of the queue and placed our papers on the counter.

The immigration official looked at the three sets of papers and told us, "One at a time," handing back Baby's and mine. He signalled us to step back behind the yellow line before he would proceed with Sheena's papers. We stepped back, pushing the others who had already moved forward, like a freight train in a shunting yard. Five minutes later our papers were stamped and we were through. We had just left the Philippines.

Manila airport was not big. There were maybe a dozen or so shops selling local products from dried mango and other fruit to miniature jeepneys and giant cigars. And there was the inevitable collection of refreshment stalls. Sheena found the duty-free shops much to her delight. None of us had any money but certainly enjoyed sampling the various perfumes. One of the assistants asked in a not too polite voice if we wanted to buy anything. Sheena finished spraying perfume on one of her wrists and commented lightheartedly that they were all so nice it was impossible to purchase just one. We laughed our way out of the shop.

* * *

The boarding gate was chaotic: people pushing to find out why there was a delay, airline staff talking into phone sets, businessmen insisting they had a connecting flight. With all this going on I wondered how they kept track of what was happening. We three stared out of the window at the huge aeroplane which dwarfed the workers standing beneath. Could it really get off the ground? Filled with anticipation and excitement, we eventually were called to board the plane and duly followed the other travellers, each vying to be first through the door.

The lady at the desk had done her best and Sheena and I were next to each other at the back of the plane with Baby in the row in front. We began flipping through the duty-free catalogue. Around us, others struggled to store their baggage and claim their seats. Sheena pinched me and said, "Here we go." I leaned over to look out the window, but other than what appeared to be several small men running around I could see nothing. When Baby turned around to talk to us, the lady next to me realised that we were all together and offered her seat to Baby.

I felt a tingle of delight as the plane pushed backward away from the terminal building. We watched as the safety demonstration was given. Seatbelts were proving to be a little bit of a problem, then the stewardess nudged the buckle and said softly: *"Huwag kayong mag-alaala walang problema,"* meaning "It's fine, relax, it will be all right."

We were all trying to get the best view out of the tiny window as the plane turned and headed for the runway. The captain asked the crew to take their seats and moments later the engines roared, brakes were released and the plane lurched forward. We all held one another's hands and squeezed, saying a little prayer. There was no turning back now. Faster and faster, the plane sped down the runway; the airport buildings seemed to rush by in the opposite direction. My stomach dropped as the plane lifted itself into the air. Two or three more thuds and the wheels tucked themselves in, and we watched the ground slip away beneath us. Then the white mist of the clouds covered our view. Manila was no more, lost below as the plane pushed higher and higher. Baby was almost sitting on my lap as she stretched her neck looking through the window.

By the time the meal arrived, we were hungry and would not have cared what was served. Sheena and I chose the chicken and noodles and Baby, the fish with rice. Sheena asked for another roll as the stewardess passed the trays. We felt like princesses picking our way through the salad and fruit dish that came with the tray. We refused wine, settling for orange juice and coffee.

We all put on headsets to listen to music while we ate dinner. Then the television screen lit up before us and a short film was shown. Nobody had told me there was television. Feverishly we flicked through the channels until the sound matched the picture. I sat there and stared; this was really living. I accepted another cup of coffee, slid the chair back and looked across, first at Sheena and then at Baby. Both had their eyes glued to the screen. I closed my eyes for a moment to store the experience, for I did not know when I would do this again and wanted to remember it forever.

The pilot announced that we were flying at thirty-seven thousand feet. As far as feet go, I had been no higher than the second floor of the promotion building, so sitting up here on the clouds watching the sea and little black dots that were ships down below, it could have been to the top of the world.

I thought the sky above my village was blue, but up here looking across a blanket of white was a blue line that curved the horizon. A pale blue that grew stronger and darker as it moved away from the curve above the plane. It was like water dropped onto a page of blue paint and watching expanding circles of deepening shades of blue. How I wished

I could take a picture of this blue paradise to show my family.

There was a quiet "whoosh" and I felt my stomach move up inside me as we started our descent. Till then I had not noticed any real turbulence. The stewardesses moved about with urgency, collecting the last of the trays and telling a few of the passengers it was too late for another drink. Sheena squeezed past us to go to the toilet, and when she returned, she showed me her souvenir: a little bottle of scented water had just "disappeared" from the toilet.

"We will share it later," she said, zipping up her bag. Already some mischief, even before the flight was over.

Already strapped in, we again grabbed hold of one another's hands and then strained our necks at the window to see as much of the world below us as we could possibly manage. I could make out some small islands and wondered which one was Hong Kong. How stupid I was. I found out later they were only small, uninhabited islands around the Hong Kong coastline. The plane banked steeply to the right and the whole of Hong Kong suddenly appeared in the window and my stomach seemed to be pushed to the left. Baby and I gasped in amazement, then a few seconds later it was gone again as the plane levelled for the landing. There were two bumps, then the engines roared and we were forced forward in our seats as land and boats sped past the window. As our plane slowly taxied to its holding place I said another prayer of thanks.

Even before the plane stopped the passengers started their dash once again. It seemed everybody was in a hurry. Chinese chatter sounded so high-pitched. I wondered not only about how much Chinese I would have to speak but also whether my English would be good enough to speak to people with such different accents.

Bags were being pulled from the lockers and people were jostling to get nearer the doors. We could see the other group of girls on the opposite side of the plane, smiling and chatting furiously. Eventually the doors opened and the people shuffled out. When there was a little space and order in the aisle, we collected our things and followed the rest.

We had been well rehearsed about what to do upon arriving. A phone number had been given to us if there was a problem with immigration. None of us had any Hong Kong money and we had not thought to ask how we could have made that call. We followed the crowd along a carpeted corridor and I could see windows on one side facing out to the tarmac. In the distance I could see several planes parked and buses taking people out to them. On the other side were huge advertisements framed in silver cases showing famous sites in Hong Kong. Those written in Chinese were like riddles. How could anyone read those squiggles? At the end of the corridor, beyond the illuminated yellow signs and black arrows, we entered a hallway and faced the line of immigration desks.

We breezed through immigration and picked up our cases, which were already going around on the carousel. This was only my second time in an airport, but even I noticed how organised Kai Tak was. There were signs, baggage carts were freely available and everything looked so new and modern.

One of the girls from the other group was laughing as they appeared through the sliding door that led from the customs area. A customs guard had asked her to open her bag only to find mostly underwear and a small teddy bear.

"I need something to cuddle at night," she told the man. He smiled and stuffed the bear back into the bag, waving them through.

We followed the taxi sign as instructed, and as we passed through the automatic doors the heat and moist, humid air swept over us, and we were faced with hundreds of people all searching through the arrival crowd for their friends. Several men were holding big signs with handwritten names. Sheena spotted ours and waved. Edna had given us the name of our contact and told us that under no circumstances were we to leave the airport without him. There was no chance of this happening as we were half-dazed and completely clueless as to how to proceed beyond the exit sign. He pointed to us to follow him and we pushed our way through the crowd.

"Welcome, my name Johnny, please follow me." Johnny was Chinese and spoke in broken English. He had a slight build and with his half-combed hair looked like he had just been sleeping.

"Is it always hot like this?" Sheena asked.

"Don't worry, you get comfortable," he replied.

We followed Johnny down the short slope. The long line of people with loaded baggage carts looked endless, but eventually it split into two as passengers moved to the left or to the right to wait for a taxi. As we approached the main queue, I viewed a sea of red taxis nudging forward to pick up passengers. Airport staff in clearly marked coats were busy retrieving empty baggage carts and returning them to the terminal building.

We piled into two taxis. Our small bags fitted easily into the trunk of our taxi. I noticed the trunks of other taxis propped open but tied down with straps because their passengers had suitcases that were too large. When I became more familiar with Hong Kong taxis, I realised that almost without exception they had at least one plastic bucket and cleaning materials stashed away in the trunk, which reduced the room they might have otherwise had for passengers' luggage.

Johnny gave the other taxi driver instructions. We sat back to enjoy our first real view of Hong Kong from ground level. The first thing that grabbed our attention was that there must have been at least as many cars on the road as in Manila, but there was an absence of noise. There was no frustrated hooting of the car horn, no black oily smoke coming from exhausts and the vehicles moved in an easy flow. Cars actually stopped when the traffic lights turned red, instead of making a quick dash through, and some cars even stopped to let other cars turn onto the road. There were so many cars and yet there was order. Several pale blue and cream coloured buses were speeding along the road, and they were two floors high! I had never seen a vehicle like this except as a toy. I saw people sitting upstairs, high above the traffic, and thought they must have a wonderful view.

Looking up at the tall apartment blocks that lined the road leading to a cross-harbour tunnel, I could see hundreds of television aerials strapped to the rooftops. Washed clothes dangled from every window and signs painted on the sides of buildings advertised cigarettes and beer. My eyes were still absorbing everything when we plunged down into the tunnel. I had not yet figured out that Hong Kong referred to more than Hong Kong Island and the airport was in Kowloon. When we came out of the tunnel, we were on Hong Kong Island and the scenery had changed. I was surrounded now by huge towering office blocks and hotels. Even stretching my neck from the car window to see how far they reached into the sky, I could not see the top of some of the buildings.

Johnny pointed to a blue and white road sign: "North Point and Quarry Bay. That's where you will be staying," he said, confirming it was Quarry Bay.

On our left was the harbour and beyond that the airport. Another jet was screaming its way along the runway, surging up into the almost cloudless sky. I watched until it disappeared from view and thought how far away the Philippines seemed right now. Hong Kong appeared to be a collection of buildings, standing side by side and going on forever. Having looked up Hong Kong in an old atlas, it appeared as a dot on the map, whereas the Philippine Islands seemed so large. Hong Kong now seemed enormous.

We pulled off from the main road and entered an area of small shops and apartment blocks. The taxi stopped and we got out, stretched and looked around. The other taxi arrived a few minutes later and Johnny paid the fare.

It was a narrow street with several small shops on both sides. Above the shops rose a line of apartments from one end of the street to the other. They looked dingy and their small windows had iron bars. There were small potted flowers and shrubs on some of the window ledges, clearly an attempt to brighten the front of the building. It was certainly a varied sight, with the mixture of shop signs and street stalls. I took a deep breath. The air smelt different but I couldn't describe it. It seemed thicker or heavier in some way, unlike the air in the Philippines. Maybe it was the surrounding harbour or the closeness of the buildings. I picked up my bag and followed the others through a green door and up a few steps to a small reception area where hundreds of post boxes lined the walls.

5. Deep Waters

Hong Kong is a city designed by nature and crafted by human hands. Possessing one of the most perfect harbours, the city is protected from the open sea and surrounded by deep water. Scarcity of land has necessitated the erecting of tall buildings, which rise quickly from the shoreline before being buttressed by tall green hills that form a natural backdrop. The infrastructure of Hong Kong provides evidence of foreign influence coupled with the industriousness of Chinese hands.

THE DAY HAD been filled with so many new experiences, I had not noticed being tired. But following Johnny through the lobby, I felt the aching in my arms and legs. One more new experience awaited us. Johnny signalled for us to enter the elevator, and we squeezed ourselves and our bags in. Johnny pressed "8" on the line of buttons and as the door closed the elevator lurched upward with a jolt. I grabbed Sheena's hand in reaction; she smiled in reassurance but I could see the worried faces of the others in their reflections on the metal walls. With a whirr and another jolt, the door opened and we squeezed out. We followed Johnny to a white door with a "B" on it. I desperately wanted to see our new home and the others must have felt the same because we created a bottleneck in the doorway. Sheena pushed us from behind, and like a cork popping from a bottletop, we half fell and stumbled into the room, bags falling to the floor.

Rose, our Filipina "house-mum", emerged from the kitchen upon hearing our noisy entrance. She greeted us in Tagalog.

"I will be here to look after you and the apartment," she said, as she wiped her hands on a towel and observed our nervous faces. "Mimi, your mamasan, will see you on Sunday." She paused as if she had forgotten what to say.

"So what do we do till then?" asked one of the girls.

"Just relax for today and get settled in. On Saturday afternoon Johnny will take you around and show you where the bars are in Wan Chai." Then, as if remembering something forgotten, she plunged her hand into her dress pocket and brought out an envelope.

"Here is some money," she said. "You can use it to buy food for the next two days." Fishing around in her other pocket, she produced two sets of keys. "Take these for now. Mimi will give you all full sets later." Before turning to leave she added, "The bedrooms are through there, so help yourself."

The lounge area was small and sparsely furnished with an old sofa and soft chairs with a table in the centre. The television sitting on the wooden sideboard was a nice surprise, as was the fan standing in the opposite corner. There was a hallway leading from the lounge to the bedrooms. Six of us took over one bedroom, the other four moved in with the two other girls already in residence. I selected my bed above Sheena's, and Baby took the top bunk next to mine. Lying on the top bunk, I could peer out the window to the street below and felt pleased with my selection.

At last we tasted freedom. We could now stay up as late as we wished and even read something in bed with the light on, a small pleasure unavailable at home or in Angeles City at the promotion. We were allowed to buy snacks and store drinks in the apartment refrigerator, but we soon learned that even putting your name on an item did not prevent it from disappearing.

Rose was our cook and house cleaner. She didn't prepare breakfast though, so if we wanted something during the morning we had to either cook it ourselves or go out to one of the Chinese coffee shops nearby. Most of the girls did not get up till noon and then went for "breakfast" at one of the small neighbourhood shops. On our first two mornings in Hong Kong, we were up earlier than the other girls in the apartment and ventured out on our own. These were fascinating outings. We ordered Chinese food by pointing to items on a menu without speaking a single word of Chinese. The waitresses appeared not to speak English. As time went on and we became more adventurous, we amazed our taste buds with all the different foods. Compared with our somewhat mundane selection of food back home, it was pure luxury to have such variety. The photographs of dishes shown on restaurant menus made everything look exciting.

Our first Chinese meal was a pleasant adventure. We plied our wooden chopsticks much to the amusement, I'm sure, of the other patrons. Every time one of us managed to pick up a piece of chicken or some noodles or rice, the others would stare to see if we could succeed in transferring it to the mouth. And almost every time it would fall off. Sheena kept using her fingers to rescue pieces of chicken. We had not had so much fun in ages. We managed to clear all the food, although looking at the table you would have thought that we had been throwing it at one another. Even the Chinese tea, which tasted strange but pleasant, was an adventure. It seemed almost impossible to get the top off the teapot to add hot water without burning your fingers.

What a sight it was to see diners digging into dishes while engaged in frenetic conversation. Waitresses moved quickly and the patrons ordered and ate quickly. One man must have grown up with chopsticks in his hand, so expertly was he scooping rice from the bowl into his mouth a few inches away. We watched him for more than a minute. He never missed and got every grain of rice. "We will be like that before we leave Hong Kong," said Sheena as we got up to leave. The door lady bowed and said "m'goy sai" as we stepped outside. We said "thank you" in return, and convinced that we had understood our first Chinese words, we slapped each other in triumph.

On both Saturday and Sunday we explored the neighbourhood. The shops were amazing. There were food shops, one or two small clothes shops, a photo developer, and stores selling Chinese medicines. We stopped to look inside at jars containing weird roots soaking in syrup-like liquid. Wooden boxes full of herbs gave off strange smells while other boxes contained what looked like bones, and deer antlers hung from pieces of string. Several customers were having their orders weighed and wrapped in white paper. Sheena said she hoped none of us got ill. We giggled and walked on. Near the end of the street we found a 7-Eleven store. Inside were products we were more familiar with including a variety of instant cup noodles. Cheap and easy to prepare, these would become one of our favourites. And of course we noticed the public phone in the store. This, we were told, could be used to make long distance telephone calls.

Without realising it, I found myself observing the Chinese going about their daily lives. I saw an old lady dressed entirely in black and bent over almost double, pushing a small trolley. It was piled high with cardboard boxes and stacks of old newspapers bundled tightly together, and plastic bags filled with old drink cans were tied to the side. The load must have been heavy, but she pushed with great determination over bumps and other road imperfections. Around market areas, things did not get thrown away, they get reused. These old ladies made their living from other people's throwaways, self-appointed "street cleaners" searching through waste bins, pulling out anything that could be recycled. It seemed odd that it was mostly old women who carried on this occupation. I felt a little sadness. Perhaps their husbands had passed away and this was all that was left for them, to scratch out a living.

We strolled aimlessly up and down the narrow streets of shops and market stalls. We must have walked for miles, yet I was not tired. This really was a wondrous place, for everywhere we turned there was something new to see. As the day wore on, more and more people came out with portable stalls and set up shop. These, I learned, were illegal hawkers who played cat-and-mouse games with the police. When the police strolled by, the vendors covered their goods and wheeled their barrows away, followed in line by all the other stallholders. Finding an alternative place, they would again set up shop and passers-by would flock over to judge the bargains. For those hawkers who sold particularly enticing products like imitation designer watches, interested customers would swarm around the stalls. It reminded me of bees surrounding an intruder at the entrance to their hive. I guess these customers were welcome intruders. And judging by the number of customers spending money at these stalls, hawkers must have found it worth the risk.

We stopped in another small coffee shop to rest for a while and indulged ourselves with a cool soft drink. We just sat and watched the world go by. I wished it could stay like this forever and that I had enough money not to have to worry. Why had I been born into a poor family? Why could I not have been one of the luckier ones, such as those passing by? I bet they could stop and drink or eat whatever they liked, whenever they wanted. Then, as if God had heard me, I saw a young legless boy who could have been no older than me. He was squatted on a small square wooden trolley. Using his hands wrapped in cloth, he pushed himself along. I looked to the sky and said "sorry". I did not share my thoughts with the others but made a point from then on to enjoy all the little moments of pleasure I could find and to be thankful for them.

* * *

On Saturday afternoon Johnny turned up to show us around. First he pointed out the main roads and the best place to get a taxi. Taxis, he told us, cannot just stop anywhere, and must be waited for in certain places. One of the best places was just along King's Road, near the Quarry Bay MTR station. He then took us on the MTR, the local underground. None of us had experienced anything like this. Flying had been one thing and now I was being driven around in a train that runs through tunnels under the ground. But before the MTR itself we had to negotiate our first scare—the escalator. This was the first time we had seen one. Some of the girls were holding on for dear life, afraid of being eaten up at the bottom as the steps disappeared into the floor. This may sound silly to people who grew up with escalators, elevators, flushing toilets and so on, but to those of us from the province, our first encounter of these things scared us.

At first we heard the train and felt the air move, then the train came rushing out from the tunnel, pushing the wind in front of us as if an underground typhoon was coming our way. The doors whooshed open. We stepped in and they whooshed shut. More than one of us was hanging onto the handrails as the train picked up speed and plunged into the dark tunnel. We could see Wan Chai on the map above the doors and we counted each station. I noticed that each station was tiled in a different colour. Every time we stopped, a stream of people got off only to be replaced by others getting on. It was like clockwork: whoosh, people got off and people got on, then whoosh, doors closed and we rushed into the darkness again. I had no idea how far we had travelled, but it seemed very quick. We could see through to all the other carriages as the train snaked its way through the tunnel. When I wrote home I was going to have so much to tell.

A prerecorded voice announced in Chinese and then in English that Wan Chai was the next stop. We got off and followed Johnny. There were so many exits and stairways. I know that by ourselves we would have been lost. Following Johnny's instructions, we put our plastic tickets into the exit machine, watched them disappear and passed through the exit.

Johnny led us along a green-tiled corridor and up flights of stairs, emerging from the station onto Lockhart Road, another busy place with people fighting their way up and down the sidewalk. Once our eyes had adjusted to the brightness, we saw the bar signs hanging out over the road and wondered at once which one we would be working in.

"Don't worry," Johnny said, seeing our eyes searching out the signs. "All the bars for this promotion are here on opposite sides of the road, so once you have found one it's easy to find the rest."

Lockhart Road in the daytime is one thing, but at night it is a totally different place as we were to discover the very next evening. The bars we passed in the light of the afternoon were shuttered, so we could not see inside them. I counted over a dozen but I'm sure I missed some. I realised then how little I knew about bars. If there were at least fifteen on this road, how many girls were there in each, and were they all from the same promotion? Johnny had said "for this promotion", so how many other promotions were supplying these bars? With so many bars to supply, this would explain why there were always so many girls training at the promotion. It was something that had puzzled me before and now it was partly answered. The limited length of stay for each girl and the sheer number of bars was one reason for the constant stream of girls going through the promotions. I had heard from others that some girls working in the bars came from Thailand, but they tended to be kept in separate apartments. Something else intrigued me. Were Len and his colleagues responsible for all this? Was it owned by Chinese? Johnny had indicated that there were other bars on streets beyond Lockhart Road.

He led us up a series of steps to a bridge crossing the main road. I could see we were heading for a huge shopping complex. As we crossed the road using this footpath in the sky, I saw strange short trains clanking along rails set into the road. The funny thing was that each train was connected to a wire running above the train by a long arm sticking up from its roof. It reminded me of a stem that sticks up from an apple to connect it to a tree branch. These trains, called trams, were not only the oldest and cheapest form of mass transport on Hong Kong Island but also the most colourful, each one painted a different colour and marked with advertising. Maybe these trams were the jeepneys of Hong Kong.

"This is Pacific Place, one of the big shopping malls," Johnny said. As we stepped out of the heat, it was like stepping into another world. Our jaws dropped for a few minutes at the sight in front of us. To our left, right and above us were some four floors of shops, layer upon layer. Artificial trees and flowers covered the walkways paved in marble. It was spotlessly clean and completely air-conditioned. *Is this one of the great shopping centres of the world?* I wondered. *Would I ever have the opportunity to shop here?*

We stopped to look in the shop windows and were busy trying to convert the prices into pesos. Johnny just kept on walking and we had to keep moving for fear of losing him. "On to Central District," he said. He was taking us to another shopping area called World Wide Plaza. And he assured us it would be more in our price range, a place where so many of the overseas Filipinos, including the thousands of maids, met to shop or pass the time of day on holidays or their days off.

As we walked, I realised that we were getting from one place to another using covered walkways suspended above the traffic. Eventually we emerged into the open, and down a flight of steps we stood in front of a white building with black lettering on its roof: Furama Hotel.

"Straight on down this road," Johnny said, never slackening his pace. We passed Chater Garden, the well-known meeting place of the Filipino community, which was, as I would find out later in my stay, was densely crowded on Sundays.

A few buildings past the Mandarin Hotel, and we had arrived. Indeed World Wide Plaza was not as impressive as Pacific Place, but it was certainly friendlier. We could hear the Filipino dialects all around us. I saw some shops with Philippine products on display, even newspapers, though they were a day or so out of date. Johnny stopped by a row of shops advertising foreign currency exchange rates.

"These shops here do money transfers direct to your home address in the Philippines." We looked around at the shops displaying exchange rates.

"This one here," he pointed and acknowledged a wave from the man behind the counter, "is a friend of mine, so if you want to send money back, tell him you work with me and you won't get ripped off." When I had learned more about the bars, the girls and their money, I would again think about his remark and wonder how much commission he got out of all the money we girls sent back home.

"Right, we will get a taxi back from here," he said as he led us outside once again.

* * *

Despite homesickness, our first few days in Hong Kong were good. You could see this by the smiles on our faces. But every time you think things are getting better, something comes along and shatters the moment. When we got back from our afternoon excursion on Sunday, Rose was waiting for us. She told us to remain in the lounge and disappeared to wake Mimi. The two girls who were already occupying the apartment greeted us but did not remain.

A lady wrapped in a silk dressing gown walked in, sat, rubbed her eyes and started. She spoke English with a Chinese accent. "My name is Mimi and I am in charge of the girls who live in this apartment." As our mamasan, she would be responsible for us whether in the bar or in the apartment. She proceeded through her long list of rules and something told me she had been through them many times before. We would be expected to get ourselves to and from the bar. Taxi was the preferred means of transport as they did not want their girls all dressed up on the buses or the MTR. Being dressed up would make us stand out next to the businessmen and regular working women. That increased our chances of being questioned by the police or "distracted" by a male admirer.

"Johnny has shown you around and I expect you to know where you are as well as how to get to the bars and back here by yourselves." Sheena's eyes lighted at the thought of freedom but the flame was short-lived.

"Don't get any ideas of disappearing by yourselves. You will be signed in and out of both here and the bar. When you leave Rose or I will inform the bar you're on your way. The bar will do the same when you return." She paused. "Any girl who disappears will be fined." There goes that awful word, I thought.

"You will not have boyfriends, at any time." She sounded just like Edna. Our working hours were from nine in the evening and that meant being in the bar, dressed and ready to dance until five in the morning. We could get changed in the bar if we liked. This way we looked more or less like anybody else during our journey to work.

"When the navy is in town," she continued, "we will be in the bar from two in the afternoon right through till five a.m."

Someone asked how often the navy visited. "Quite regularly. But don't worry," she added, "we always know in advance when they are coming."

Some days we would be allowed to go home at two a.m., provided there were enough girls remaining in the bar. This would be on a rotational basis. If we were late for work or not properly dressed we could expect to be fined. She would explain how this worked later.

I was beginning to feel like a prisoner once again, but there was more to come. One girl interrupted her to ask if we got a day off.

"You work seven days a week."

We would have to buy our costumes from her and she had many to choose from. Girls that had finished their tour sold them back, so we would have a chance to select from these hand-me-downs at a very good price. In addition, we must wear two pairs of tights while we were dancing.

She told us that the police were very strict.

"No hair," pointing between her legs. "No hair must be showing. That's why you wear two pairs."

Again, we could buy these tights from her to start with. We would also be fined if we had holes in our tights. She did not want her girls to look scruffy.

"You must also buy at least one shirt to wear over your shoulders when you're not dancing." If we left the bar to sit with a customer, we had to slip a shirt over our top. I wondered how soft and flimsy a costume must be to show more than what would be allowed.

As far as our freedom was concerned there was to be little. We were booked in and out of the apartment and were not allowed out by ourselves, even in groups. On the odd occasion when we needed to go to the shops, it would have to be with her express permission and only for the time specified, normally one hour. She made it sound as if she was doing us a great favour.

"I know you have to buy things—napkins, makeup and so on, but ask me first. If I find you out by yourself without permission you will be fined."

The only exception was if we went out in small groups for breakfast or lunch, but even then if we stayed out too long it would be noted.

"Now to your salary." We all paid attention. She told us we would be paid 3,500 Hong Kong dollars each month. On top of that if we had earned commissions from drinks or bar fines, these would be paid at the same time. I quickly calculated that the salary was, at the current exchange rate, over 10,000 pesos. It had a nice sound. Then came some more news. Our accommodation and food cost was 1,000 Hong Kong dollars per month and we would be expected to share the electricity bill.

"So," she pointed at the electric fan, "if you choose to use the fan, remember it comes out of your salary." We all looked at the fan spinning round, but no one got up to turn it off.

"As for the bill you incurred at the promotion, I have not received that yet, but as soon as I do, part of it will be deducted each month and sent to the manager." None of us knew how much our bill was or how much would be deducted each month. I did not even want to think of it. She was still pouring out the rules.

"If you have any fines," she stopped and looked at us, "these will also be deducted." Faces that had been smiling just a short time ago were now frowning.

"As far as the apartment is concerned, I expect you to keep it clean, and I will check every now and then." We would be expected to do our own washing and could ask Rose to buy soap from the market for us, but we had to pay for it. "And don't have all your wet washing hanging around all over the place." We should keep our washing in the bathroom or in our bedrooms. "When you have your period, don't leave your napkins in the bathroom. Throw them away." Her voice indicated that this was another one of her pet hates.

She would bring in the costumes the next day for us to buy.

"We don't have any money left," lamented one of the girls.

"Don't worry. You will find that all the mamas will make you a loan and you can pay it back from your salary."

I had visions of my 3,500 dollar salary getting smaller and smaller.

"If ever you want to borrow some money, just ask me. You will need some to start you off to pay for the taxis."

Before she finished, she told us that we would visit the bars that night. I looked at Sheena and Baby. I knew we all hoped to be in the same bar. With that she stood up, tightened the belt on her dressing gown and returned to her bedroom.

* * *

Sheena told Baby and me to follow her. She went off into the bedroom where the other two girls were. She introduced us and we chatted for a while, talking about all the rules we had just been given.

"Is it really true about the fines?" asked Sheena.

"Everything the Mama said is true. She's very strict."

"And if you sneak out, Rose will tell on you," added the other girl.

"How much are fines?" Sheena asked.

"Depends on the situation and her mood," said the first girl. "Late for work, 200 to 1,000 dollars. Goes up if you've been late before. Costume dirty or you turn up at the bar without one, 500 the first time and maybe 1,000 if it happens again. Go out from the apartment or late coming back, a straight 500."

"There's no point in arguing," cautioned the second girl. "It will just make it worse for you next time."

"Borrowing means adding 50 to 100 Hong Kong to the total when it's time to repay," volunteered the first girl.

With all these fines and payments, I thought there would be nothing left of my 3,500 dollars. Yet if that was the case, why were all these girls here? They must be making some money. Much later, I would learn that by keeping us poor and knowing our families were desperate for money, the mamas could pressure us into going out on bar fines, which is where most of their money was made. But that first Sunday, I was still innocently thinking that dancing and drinking were going to provide a nice little income for my family and me.

* * *

It was around six o'clock and Rose was preparing dinner. The other two girls were getting changed to go to the bar. "We normally leave here around seven thirty," one of them said. The other added, "Sometimes it's difficult to get a taxi."

Most of us had flopped down and kicked off our shoes. I for one was not used to all that forced walking and my feet ached.

"I'm going to take a shower," said Sheena.

I picked up a rather worn Tagalog magazine and started to read. One of the others turned on the television.

Glancing at the magazine made me think of the Philippines and something my father had said. "When you get to Hong Kong, phone your Auntie Tina and say hello." Tina was from my mother's side. I had seen pictures of her but we had never met. She had moved to Hong Kong many years ago and was still here working as a domestic helper. The thought spurred me into action and I went to my room to get her number.

Even though Rose helped me dial the number, this was my first phone call and a strange feeling of sophistication came over me.

Tina was so surprised to hear from me, and after I had explained who I was we spent some twenty minutes talking about our family and relatives. She gave me her address, which I wrote on the piece of paper, and said that we must keep in touch. Sunday was her only day off. I explained I had to work seven days a week. "Never mind," she said. "Phone me when you can and I will try and meet you one lunchtime." She sounded very sweet and it was nice to know that I had family here who was not part of the bar scene. I folded the paper with her address and number on it, and returned it to my bag.

* * *

We were all exhausted and sat around sluggishly. About an hour later, Mimi reappeared from her room and said, "After dinner tonight, I want you all to get changed into jeans and a *clean* tee shirt. Remember, I will be taking you to your bars." Again, the three of us looked at each other with the same thought, *would we be together?* She continued, "I want you to just sit in the bar where I leave you and watch. Do not talk to *anyone*. The other mamas know you are coming, so they will keep an eye on you."

Unable to contain myself, I asked, "Which bars will we work in?"

"I will give you the details later, but there are three bars where you will be working and you will see them all tonight: San Francisco Club, Club Carnival and Country Club." I could see she was not going to give any more away, so I left it and said another short prayer.

"Don't forget," she added, "I will be back here at nine thirty." She looked around and repeated, "Nine thirty, so make sure you're all here." She headed off to her room. "Oh, one more thing," she said, turning at the door. "Put a little makeup on, but not too much."

"Won't be long now," said Sheena.

"What do you mean?"

"The bars—won't be long till we see them and then tomorrow we will be working in one of them."

Ever since we arrived in Hong Kong I had noticed that Sheena was getting more and more excited at the prospect of working in the bars and earning some money. I was happy to be here and pleased that we had all managed to stay together so far, but the thought of working in the bar still unsettled me.

My thoughts turned to the two other girls in our apartment. They seemed happy. I noticed they had new clothes, a watch each and they always seemed to have nice makeup. I put my old fears out of my mind. Today had been such a nice day, barring the lecture from Mimi. I did not want to spoil it.

Eight o'clock and the apartment was abuzz with activity. We were all determined to be ready well ahead of time. None of us wanted to upset Mimi. Sheena splashed on some of the scented water she had taken from the airplane and passed the bottle to me. I dabbed some on and handed it to Baby. She did the same and handed it back. Sheena put it back in her bag. "It won't last long if they all use it," she said as she zipped it up.

Nine thirty came and went and Mimi had not reappeared. We waited patiently for another ten minutes or so, then she made her entrance.

"Come on then." She walked past us to the door. "Let's get going."

We followed her out and down the steps to find a taxi. How was she going to get us all into one taxi? As soon as we got to the pavement a minibus conveniently pulled up alongside the curb. It belonged to a friend of Johnny's and Mimi had reserved it for the evening's tour.

6. Eyes of the Night

Older Hong Kong streets are a maze of advertising and famous for their jumbled array of stick-like signs jutting out from building walls. Because buildings are tightly spaced and offices located far above the ground, these signs compete for the passer-by's attention. As day becomes night, signs visible in daylight fade into obscurity, giving way to lit signs. Perhaps nowhere are the lights so prominent as on Lockhart Road in Wan Chai. Lining both sides of the street, the go-go bars create for the bar-goer an artificial daylight. These lights are the eyes of the night.

I THINK THAT the most outstanding impression for anyone coming from a poor, rural background, where electricity is a luxury, must be the multitude of lights that are everywhere in Hong Kong. I could see a few from my apartment bedroom, but driving along and seeing so many was another truly amazing sight that I will always remember. Lights large and small. Some appeared to be blinking away and changing colours, others were just bright and static. Some hung out over the roads, others perched on top of buildings. The combination was breathtaking.

I lost track of time, absorbed with the splendour of the Hong Kong night. The road we pulled into was again full of lights. The names on some of the signs I recognised as the bars. We were in Lockhart Road.

Stepping out of the minibus, I stood and looked around at a sight that was going to face me every night for the foreseeable future. It looked so bright and exciting. And it was just as busy now as it was earlier in the day, fuelled by a constant stream of taxis dropping people off and picking others up.

* * *

"We will start in Carnival Club." The doorman pulled back the blue velvet curtains and we followed Mimi in. Like the other clubs, the bars had no doors, just curtains that parted in the middle.

The bar was dimly lit except for the stage illuminated by small flashing ceiling lights. I counted quickly, seven girls on stage. They dressed much the same, in swimsuits and high-heeled shoes or knee-high black boots. Where were the costumes? And what about the dance routines? For a brief, silly minute, I thought a mistake had been made. Then I realised that the next day one of these girls would be me. I was frozen to the spot, hardly believing what I saw. I looked at Sheena, then at Baby, trying to read their thoughts. The bar had a number of booths, small semicircular cubicles set back from the main stage with soft sofa-like seats. They spread around two sides of the main stage. Mimi asked us to sit down, and I turned my attention back to the girls on the stage. They smiled at us in a way that indicated they had seen it all before, and went on exchanging comments, no doubt about us "new girls". They wore a lot of makeup. I wondered how they could use all those colours and make it look so neat.

I had mixed feelings of shock and relief. Relieved at how big the bar was and how many girls were working there. And shocked at how they were dancing—freestyle, with no choreography, to music that blended one sound into the other. *So why did we go through all of those dance routines back in Angeles City? Why all that training?* I don't know whether it was the swimsuits that bothered me as much as the idea that this whole thing was a scam. What about Arnie, the dance routine and the POEA? So I was here and would be expected to do what I was now observing on stage in front of me. Swimsuits were one thing but boots and suspenders quite another. I looked again around the bar. Seven or eight customers were drinking but it was hardly busy. Perhaps it was still too early. One of the girls sat at the bar with a customer, a drink in her hand, talking away. I looked at Baby, who also seemed confused; then I glanced across to Sheena, whose face said "Let me get up and dance now."

After a while Mimi summoned us and we proceeded to the Country Club across the road. Again she placed us in some spare seats, then disappeared to talk with the other mamas. Club Carnival was completely circular and the barstools formed a dotted perimeter. All of this gave the impression of being larger, with more space for the girls to move around. But at Country Club, the girls danced in a line on a single-side stage, with mirrors across the back. In that limited space, there was only room to wiggle to the music, occasionally swapping positions. Also, the bar was narrow, leaving little room between the customers and the girls sitting around in front of the stage. It looked as though the customer could stand up and reach out in any direction and touch the girls. I hoped I would not be working here. Baby and Sheena were also not impressed by this setup.

Mimi again collected us and took us out. As I held Baby's hand, she said, "Hope I am not in there." I squeezed her hand and said another prayer. It was only a short walk up the road to San Francisco Club. Again, there was a doorman who lifted the curtain, this time a red velvet one. This bar was similar to Club Carnival in its layout. It was not as big, but the stage was an oval. The bar wrapped itself completely around, so that the girls had to enter and leave underneath a small hatch. Several small booths around two sides of the bar were occupied and a few girls were sitting in the booths. Five girls were dancing, about twice that number were seated. They smiled at us and we returned the smile. They knew that tomorrow some of us would be sitting right where they were now.

I couldn't help but notice that all the mamasans I had seen were Chinese. I could only assume that they had been bar girls back in the days before Filipinas came to Hong Kong. It seemed strange that all the dancers in these three bars were Filipina. Some, I'd heard, were Thai but I'd never heard of any dancers who were Chinese. While it came as less of a surprise to hear some of the Filipinas using Chinese, it certainly sounded unusual to hear the mamas blurting out phrases in Tagalog.

Wow, this is all different, I am here, I thought. Out of all the bars we had seen, I wanted to be in Club Carnival. To me it was larger, with more room to move around or, as I schemed, to hide from the customers. I said another prayer when I thought of the Country Club—I could not see myself dancing with that line of men staring at me, especially with the long back mirror on the stage showing even more of me to the customer. The San Francisco bar was not too bad, but I hoped Club Carnival would be mine.

By the time Mimi reappeared it was almost midnight. She took us out and told us to go straight home. She would see us at two o'clock the next day.

Nobody else asked, so I did. "Which bars will we be in?"

Hand in the air, she hailed a taxi. "I will tell you tomorrow," she said, and added, "We don't want to spoil the surprise, do we?"

Sheena, Baby, myself and two others piled into one taxi and Mimi shouted the address in Chinese: *jak yue chung, ying wong do, gau-baak-baat-sap-gau, m'goy*. The taxi pulled away, heading for 989 King's Road in Quarry Bay. I looked back and could see Mimi doing the same for the other girls.

After spending only twenty minutes in each bar, I was in a daze. Other than the physical layout, I could see little difference between them. There were girls dancing, customers drinking and mamas watching. I recalled Mama Mimi saying that she would be responsible for "us" girls, but did that mean she worked between the three different bars or were we under the control of yet another mama while at the bar? These thoughts puzzled me and I didn't notice that we had reached King's Road. Sheena paid the taxi driver, telling us that we could split it with her when we got inside.

Like a faithful watchdog, Rose was there to see us in. Now that we were all inside, she was off, telling us she would return tomorrow. Some of the girls went straight to bed; the three of us sat around.

"It won't be that bad," said Sheena, as if she could read our thoughts on our faces. "If all we have to do is dance like that, it's easy." Certainly just getting up and dancing to whatever music was playing took away the need to practise, but I had never danced by myself. "It's easy," Sheena carried on. "You just get up and wiggle your body around to the music." She demonstrated to the rest of us in an exaggerated way, proving only that it was easy for her. She had no inhibitions about looking "silly" in front of the other girls and the customers. She flopped down beside me, "Don't worry, I will be there with you." A reassuring thought, provided we would be in the same bar.

I fell asleep thinking about what we had seen. The day that had started so well now left me feeling apprehensive. Tomorrow I would be a bar girl. I would have to get up and dance with the rest of them, look like them, probably act like them. How I wish I had been born with a stronger mind, one that did not try to find problems with everything. Why could I not be more like Sheena, able to go along with things and not worry? My last thought before I dropped off to sleep was about my two friends. With them, I felt I could do it. By myself, I would be a wreck.

The morning started slowly with none of us rushing to get up. We knew it was going to be a long day and an even longer night. We counted our money and decided not to do anything special for breakfast, settling for a bowl of noodles at a small Chinese café across the road known as "Mimi's local". When we returned, Mimi was handing out the mandatory tights. They would of course be added to our bill. I was getting worried and asked Mimi about the bill from the promotion. "It will be here by next week at the latest," she told us. "So don't worry about it."

"Sheena, Baby and Mary," she called out. "You will be dancing together in San Francisco Club." My heart gave a little leap as I heard those words. I was a little disappointed that it was not Club Carnival, but glad it was not Country Club.

"You must be in the bar by eight thirty and ready to dance. Take your dance costumes with you. You will get them later this afternoon. And don't forget your tights." I looked at the other girls. Except for the two selected for Country Club, the others looked pleased. Before she returned to her room Mimi advised us to get some sleep in the afternoon.

We knew by now that Rose normally served up dinner around six thirty, so we had the whole day to do what we wanted.

"Can we go out for lunch?" Sheena asked before Mimi shut her door.

"If you like, but you will be the ones who are tired."

We thanked her, knowing it was always good to show gratitude even for small favours.

"Don't fall asleep at the bar, or you'll be asking for trouble," she added.

"This might be our last chance for a while to go out," said Sheena. "Why don't we take lunch, then sleep for an hour or so afterward?" Baby and I needed no encouragement. We grabbed our bags and left.

With little money, we opted for McDonald's. We talked about our delight at being together. So far we had been very lucky. I wondered if Edna had something to do with it but decided that she could not have been involved. Her job with us was finished.

Chicken nuggets with sweet and sour sauce might not seem like a meal to get excited about, but this was only my third McDonald's meal. Sitting with my two friends, talking about the night ahead and our dreams for tomorrow filled me with excitement. We walked back the long way, spending as much time as we could outside. None of us talked much about the bar, but I for one felt so much better knowing Sheena would be there. When we arrived back a little later, the place was deserted.

To our rooms we went, but it is hard to force yourself to sleep when your body is not tired and your mind is awake. I tossed and turned, trying to blank out all thoughts and street sounds. I closed my eyes and forced all sounds to merge into a hypnotic fuzz. Soon I was asleep.

* * *

I awoke to the noise of the apartment and the smell of cooking oil saturating the air. I could hear voices from the shower, and passing the door of the other bedroom I saw two girls brushing their wet hair. It was common for Sheena and me or Baby to shower together. Back home, my sister and I often bathed together and brushed and dried each other's hair. If the shower room had been a little larger, I think all three of us would have shared it. Sheena had already showered, so Baby and I staked our claim to be next.

We had decided as a group not to add to the electricity bill. Hot water was not needed; we were all used to taking cold showers anyway, and the fact that you could simply turn on a tap and get water from a real showerhead was pleasure enough, so having a hot shower never really entered our heads. I must admit, though, that I was tempted on occasion when the temperature fell overnight. Baby and I took turns washing, helping each other to rinse all the shampoo out of our hair. Sleep had cleansed my mind of worry and I felt fresh inside and out. This was to be our routine most nights—shower, dress in our jeans, eat dinner and then leave early for the bar. We had learned from the other girls in the apartment not to put all our makeup on in the apartment. The taxi driver would try to chat you up and the humidity would ruin it. So we followed the proven method: change and do our makeup and hair at the bar.

When I had almost finished drying my hair I heard a commotion coming from the lounge. The other girls were pulling swimsuits from a large cardboard box that Mimi had dragged from her room into the lounge. "Sort out what you need," she said, sitting down and looking at the girls kneeling around the box and digging deeper for what was underneath. There were a few tugs of war when two different hands found a nice costume. I joined in, trying to keep my towel in place. Here were our so-called costumes, a simple collection of secondhand swimsuits abandoned or confiscated by the mamas from other girls gone before.

"Make sure you have at least three," she stressed. "Customers who come back to the bar don't want to see you in the same one."

I was still struggling to find one I liked when she revealed that there was another box in her room. A few of us disappeared to find it.

Sheena went for the more daring outfits and had less competition for them. Eventually we all ended up with at least one that we liked.

I had already decided that my costume would be as plain as possible, though with each of us in need of at least three, choices were somewhat limited. I was pleased with one of my selections, a lovely turquoise with golden yellow leaves on it. It was vaguely similar to the smock dress that my mother wore on the day I left for Hong Kong.

We returned to our preparations. The place was a hive of activity and I realised just how small it was. Trying to get in front of a mirror or finding a place to change took some ingenuity. In the background I could smell the food Rose was preparing in the kitchen, but I was determined to get myself ready before I ate. Eventually the room thinned out as those girls who finished took up a seat in the lounge.

Dinner included green vegetables with rice and a small sprinkling of meat cubes. I did not feel that hungry but forced myself to eat as much as I could. I didn't know when we would eat next. Would it be five in the morning or sometime the following night? With little time to spare, we made sure our costumes, tights, makeup and hairbrushes were in our bags, then we sat down to relax.

Although four passengers appeared to be the maximum number that most Hong Kong taxis could accommodate, some took five passengers. To make our fare cheaper per person, we found two other girls to share the ride with us. Rose clocked us out as we left and I am sure she was on the phone to the bar before we had even reached the street below. It was almost dark as we crossed the road and made for the MTR station. Many of the stalls had already begun to pack up for the day, but others were just appearing. Things being sold ranged from pirated cassette tapes to imitation designer clothes. Their trade, unlike the simple daytime hawkers selling fruits and other innocent goods, seemed to require the partial protection of the night. I guess they felt safer in the dark, and in a way, so did I. I did not want other people to know what I did or where I was going. The fact that I was now a bar girl worried me a little. It was as if there was a stigma attached to working in the bar. I knew there were prostitutes in the bars, but I was not one of them.

7. Grey Puffs of Smoke

To ward off evil spirits, a Chinese mamasan would occasionally practise the ritual of burning fake money. Standing in front of her bar in early evening, she would feed colourful fake bills of enormous denominational value into small fires housed in metal tins. Even more ubiquitous were the miniature Buddhist shrines permanently installed in front of the go-go bar or located in its interior. In front of each shrine were placed sacrificial offerings of fruit, usually bananas or oranges. At the centre and back of each shrine was a red vertical sign inscribed with six black Chinese characters, "men kou tu di cai shen"—keep evil spirits out and welcome the god of money. Each sand-filled porcelain cup, in which incense sticks burned two or three at a time, was engraved with four characters to be read in pairs: "jin yu, man tang"—gold and jade are filling the temple.

Within the confines of each go-go bar, the line between spirituality and materialism blurred, not unlike the grey puffs of smoke that rose from incense sticks to blend seamlessly with the surrounding air.

WE ARRIVED AT the bar. My heart was pounding as we stepped onto the sidewalk. We wished the other two girls luck as they walked toward their bar. The old Chinese doorman sat on a small stool beside the entrance, playing with his false teeth. He smiled at us and pulled back the curtain. It was deserted except for an old Chinese lady wiping the bar with a damp cloth. I could smell stale tobacco all the way to the changing room.

The changing room was small, noisy and smelly. With no real ventilation, and the sheer number of girls, costumes, shoes, tights and clothes lying around, it was inevitable that body odour would hang in the air. Now and then, there was a welcome scent as one of the girls sprayed some perfume on her body. The room was too small for everyone to change at once and certainly not big enough for doing our makeup and hair. Mimi allocated a locker to each of us and handed us our key. She hardly had to remind us what would happen if we lost it, but took some pleasure in stressing the word "fine". Then she showed us the sign-in list.

"Sign in and out against your name. Make sure you write the time." Sheena sarcastically glanced at her bare wrist. "Failure to do so will result in fine," Mimi said, as if fearing she might be ignored. Lecture over, she told us to get changed and join the others.

Like most other girls from the province, I had never owned a swimsuit. On rare trips to the beach, we swam in shorts and tee shirt, and before we reached puberty, simply naked. Yet here I was, not going swimming but preparing to dance in swimwear and my mandatory two pairs of tights.

Putting my costume on for the first time, I examined myself in the old, cracked mirror that hung behind the door. No matter how I adjusted my shoulder straps, it just did not look like me. Sheena and Baby were pushing me to one side to glance at themselves in the mirror. Sheena looked comfortable in hers and Baby, though nervous, did look sexy.

The others were huddled in front of their makeup cases, furiously applying colours. Hair was brushed into shape and hair spray was hissing from aerosols, filling the air with sweet scent. Seeing me struggle with my hair, one of the girls, Malou, offered me her spray. "Here"—holding my fringe against my forehead—"that's better." I felt the cold spray whoosh across my face. I thanked her and sat back to watch the others. I had managed to get an old shirt from Mimi's box, choosing the largest I could find in hopes it would cover more.

It was only a quarter to nine, and the music was not too loud. Mimi came over to us and told us to watch the other girls. She was still going through her list of instructions—"smile at the customer", "look sexy on the stage", "keep asking for drinks"—when two businessmen in suits walked in, their ties undone at the collar and briefcases in their hands.

One of the girls called, "Hi, Peter, how are you?" Peter was middle-aged, with red hair and a slight build. They walked up to the bar counter and sat down.

"Does she know them?" I asked one of the girls.

"Yes, they're regulars." Then she added that the two of them pop in now and again and usually buy drinks for Amy and Fiona.

I looked over. Amy and Fiona sat across the bar pouring the two beers that had been ordered. Mimi was hovering, asking for drinks for the girls.

"In a minute, in a minute," said one of the men abruptly.

Mimi just stood there, rubbing her finger down the line of her throat, saying, "So thirsty." They ignored her and returned to their conversation.

I watched Amy and Fiona talking to each other but holding the men's hands. The girl I was talking to stood up as the music was turned up a little louder. She slipped off her shirt and stepped onto the stage. Three others around the other side of the bar did the same. Mimi came over and sat down as Baby came across to sit next to me.

"You two dance next," she said, looking straight at us.

Fear gripped me as I looked at the four girls on stage.

"Three songs dancing then you sit down."

I tried to smile an acknowledgement to Mimi. Baby rescued me by confirming that it was three songs before we sat down.

"Yes," agreed Mimi. "Just remember which group of girls you dance after. I don't want to have to remind you every time."

"Yes, Mama," we both said.

Sheena smiled and said quietly, "Don't worry, it will be okay."

Songs played from music tracks. A few I recognised but most had been jazzed up with quicker beats. The first song was soft and had a quick beat. It was called *Real Thing* and it would become Sheena's favourite. I guess the words of the song fitted her constant search for Mr Right and her neverending belief that he was out there somewhere.

I've been holding on,
I've been looking for the real thing,

Waiting patiently,
But I never stop believin',

Say I'm chasing rainbows,
Living in a dream,
Lord I kept my fantasy,
I'm never givin' in...

I had lost interest in watching Amy and Fiona and was more concerned with how many songs were played. Two to go. I was so glad there were only two men in the bar. Though they were not even looking at the dancers, I felt as if everybody else was watching me sit there. Two other mamas had arrived and introduced themselves as Mama Chee and Mama Rita. I found out later that they all tend to work together, even though girls were in fact allocated to a particular mama. The last song was almost through. Then the music stopped and the silence between songs created a pause and I froze. Baby grabbed me by the arm and pulled me up. As I stood up I instinctively slipped off my shirt and dropped it onto the seat. Baby was already on the stage with two other girls. Sheena was sitting and smiling. I lifted my leg up onto the stage and Baby helped pull me up.

Here I was standing in a swimsuit underneath the flashing lights, in front of real people. Baby held my hand and started to sway to the music. I closed my eyes, thinking of my brothers and sisters, took a deep breath and moved. I opened my eyes. Baby was smiling, still holding my hand, and Sheena was clapping silently at the two of us. I glanced down to find that none of the mamas was watching us. None of the other girls, except for Sheena, was even paying attention, and the two men were still sitting there drinking and talking. I suddenly felt like an idiot. Why had I been so frightened? What was the big deal? So what? I am dancing to music in my swimsuit and nobody cares. I let go of Baby's hand and swung my arms a little in time to the music. I was dancing.

Of the songs played, most were current pop songs. But many times I couldn't tell a brand new song from an older song that had been remixed. In the Philippines the most popular songs were soft ballads, especially the kind you could sing while visiting a roadside karaoke. Parents and children were equally familiar with these songs, which were understandably dated. In the go-go bar I was hearing new and different music, music with Latin beats, fast rhythms, hard rock themes and songs with foreign words.

I never would have remembered the first song I ever danced to because I had not really heard the music. Baby later reminded me that it was *Cross My Heart*. It had a nice disco beat and the female singer sang it in a sexy way. Baby would always dance to it most energetically— her name was in the song! All the girls had the habit of stopping and pointing at her when the singer uttered the word "baby":

You've got me head over heels,
You better believe it,
Baby,
And I love how it feels,

Cross my heart, hope to die,
May lightning strike me if I'm telling a lie...

By the time this song had finished, Mama had at last persuaded the men to buy Amy and Fiona drinks. As I watched, another man entered the bar and ordered a beer. He lit a cigarette and walked to the toilet. By the time he returned I was into my third dance. He sipped his drink and glanced around, then looked up onto the stage. The stage was indeed hard to miss, right in the centre, and the brightest spot in the whole bar. I suddenly felt self-conscious again as he looked at me. I turned so my back was facing him. There was a small pillar covered in small square mosaic mirrors at the end of the dance area with enough room for one girl to move around. I made for it, hoping to find a sanctuary. I glanced back to find he was not looking at me. The music finally stopped and it was over.

Sheena was already moving onto the stage. I hopped down and retrieved my shirt, sliding it over my arms quickly. I sat down and took a roll of toilet paper from under the bar, tearing off a few pieces to mop my forehead. I knew that the first dance had been an ordeal for Baby too. We exchanged smiles, relieved it was over, and turned to watch Sheena. She was throwing herself into the music. It was as if her big opportunity had arrived and she could celebrate it with people seeing her dance.

Looking up at Sheena, a thought rushed through my mind. What was all the fuss about learning to dance back in Angeles, when all we were expected to do now was sway to music and look sexy? I had never seen a pole in the promotion, and yet here there were three chrome poles reaching up from the stage and secured to the ceiling.

The same was true for virtually all the other bars. It was with a pole that a girl could display her talent, sliding up and down, rubbing herself against it. How stupid the promotion setup seemed, how farcical the dance routines and costumes.

Mimi was leaning on the bar in front of the newcomer, rubbing her throat and saying how thirsty she was. Not interested, he simply ignored her requests for drinks. She fanned the room with her hand, telling him to look around at all the girls. I did not know it at the time but this was a standard practice. First the mama would try to get a drink for herself, then try and get the man interested in a girl. Once she had a girl with him, she would assume he was going to buy the girl a drink and slip a drink voucher into his "pot". The pot was merely an empty plastic cup used to collect all the bills—a running tab. One type of customer the mamas did not like was the one who insisted on paying his bills as he went along. There was then less chance for the mamas to help him run up larger bills. For if the customer paid for each drink as it arrived, he would see how expensive the drinks really were. If drink vouchers were placed directly into the pot, the customer would not realise the expense until it was too late.

Then it happened. Mimi was calling for me to join them. I looked at Baby, then back at Mimi, her face showing annoyance. She beckoned to me again. Fear gripped me again as she made the introduction.

"Mary, this is Robert." She held my arm, moving my hand into his.

"Hello," he said as he took my hand. His hand was cold and large, and it wrapped itself like a leaf around mine.

"Hi," I said timidly.

"Robert is here on business, staying at the Excelsior," Mimi continued. She placed her hand on my shoulder and exerted pressure to get me to sit. I was conscious that my shirt had parted and my legs and lower body were now on full display. I moved my free hand to cover myself up but casually Mimi placed her hand on mine and held it.

He was looking me over and grinning at the exact moment Mama said, "Drink for the girl?" He nodded, still holding my hand. She whispered to me, "Don't be shy and don't cover your legs up." I tried to smile. I don't know how Mimi did it but she persuaded Robert to buy her a drink as well. Then I learned another of their tricks. She said she would buy him a beer if he bought her a drink. The difference? His beer cost about twenty-five Hong Kong dollars, but her drink cost him 110 dollars. Another slip went into the pot. She handed me a ticket when the drink arrived. This was my receipt to record that I had been bought a drink.

Mimi led the conversation, telling him I was new, asking him how long he would be in Hong Kong. I half listened, trying to smile and say a few things. He was still holding my hand, a cigarette in the other hand. I could not believe I was sitting here in front of my first customer and holding the hand of a man I had never met before. Every now and then I would glance at him, but my shyness kept me from staring. His blond hair was brushed back off his forehead and his brow was wrinkled. He had loosened his tie and undone the button on his collar. His thick neck was tanned and he wore a gold chain matching his bracelet. I noticed he smoked a lot, lighting one before the other had been put to rest.

Mimi nudged me to drink up. The drink was supposed to be vodka and Coke but it was only Coke. I was glad because I had never drunk alcohol. On good nights eager customers would buy girls several drinks. It could not be alcohol or the girls would get drunk and be unable to function in the bar. I sipped the drink a little quicker and Mimi asked him to buy another. "Last one," he said, finishing his glass. Another slip hit the pot and the conversation dragged on. I had lost count of who was dancing but Mimi told me that I was next. Even drinking with a customer did not excuse you from taking your turn on the dance stage. I suppose they thought that if a customer liked a girl, getting an even better look at her without her shirt on might be enough to have him ask her out. Baby called to me. I said, "It's my turn to dance." Robert released my hand and I returned to the other side of the bar to deposit my shirt.

Again I sought the sanctuary of the glass pillar, but Mimi was having none of it. She called me over to dance in front of Robert. I closed my eyes, breathed deeply and moved over. Swaying to the music, I soon realised that I was now holding my hands to cover my private parts. It was not intentional. I just did not know what to do with my hands. I could see Mimi's displeasure, so again I pictured my family and tried to shut out Robert, Mimi and all the others in the bar. Don't ask me how, but I suddenly found that I could look at someone watching me and not actually see him. This talent that I suddenly discovered on that first night was to help me through many occasions when I felt the stare of a man's eyes. I remembered the times that Len watched me at the promotion. If only I had been able to do it then.

At last my three dances were over and I returned for my shirt. This time I did up as many of the buttons as I could before walking back to Robert and Mimi. I sat down. He did not move to take my hand but remarked how beautiful I was. I thanked him with a blush. Mimi tried to get me another drink. He said *no*, adding that he was leaving but might return tomorrow. He finished his drink, put out his cigarette with fingers stained brown with tobacco and stood up from the barstool. I said a polite "goodnight", then he was gone. I could return to the safety of my friends. As I sat down I was shaking and my heart was still racing. I had just met my first customer.

Baby came over and asked me what we talked about. I honestly could not remember. I showed her my tickets for drink commissions. "Great," she said. I glanced up at Sheena to show off the two tickets. She stopped dancing and leaned over the stage. "Breakfast is on you," she said. Baby and I chuckled.

As the night changed to early morning, more people entered the bar. Some of them had been bar hopping and were drunk. I noticed the more experienced girls instinctively approached these customers. In between dances and serving the customers, I took time to take in the atmosphere of the bar. I had to be careful to look busy. Once or twice I noticed not only Mimi but also all the other mamas watching what we were all doing. We might be assigned to Mimi but if she was busy any one of the other mamas would take over the policing of us girls.

What I had seen from the relative safety of our first visit seemed now to emphasise the spectacle of the bars. The raised stage set under flashing lights was like an arena. Surrounding it were the customers eyeing up the prizes on display.

I was tired, my feet hurt and my eyes were sore. Wearing high-heeled shoes was much different from the trainers we had worn at the promotion. The other girls complained of aching feet as well. I wondered why we had not trained in heels. And I had only been in the bar for a few hours and my eyes were stinging from cigarette smoke. I could even smell it on my hair. It seemed that every bar-goer smoked. Only my first night and I felt like a smoked fish.

Past three o'clock, the bar was quiet. Only one or two customers remained and looked as though they would not last much longer. Girls were still dancing but nobody was paying them any attention. I asked one of the girls if it was always like this. It was fairly typical, she answered, though sometimes it was busy all night. Customers would normally start to disappear around three o'clock and those that remained were either half asleep or had stopped drinking.

Mimi said that as it was our first night we could go home early. She reminded us that going home meant straight home and warned Sheena not to lose the keys to the apartment. She said she would have keys for all of us in another day or so. I for one did not have any energy left to go anywhere other than home and I am sure the others felt the same. We changed, collected our things and left the bar. The doorman smiled and said goodnight. The night air smelt good and the absence of music was a relief. Waiting for a taxi, I could see people still walking around and the lights from the other bars still blazing. The taxi pulled up and we all slumped in. Sheena was doing her best to pronounce our address in Chinese, saying "tong chong guy" before the taxi driver turned on the light to read it from the piece of paper Baby handed him. He mumbled, noting confirmation, and off we went. The journey home was quick with no traffic to speak of. We dragged ourselves upstairs and dropped onto our beds. It was as much as I could do to climb those four small steps at the end of my bunk bed. None of us had the energy to speak—that would have to wait till morning.

* * *

That night I dreamed of my family back in my house in the Philippines. I was sitting on the sofa and they were all talking to me but I could not hear them. I saw Mimi and Robert looking up, watching me dance. I was high above them looking down from an aeroplane and yet I could see their faces clearly. Flashing, coloured stage lights lit up around my family as if they were dancing. I could smell the bar—a mixture of perfume, beer and cigarettes.

When I woke up it took me a moment to realise where I was. I lay there gathering my senses, still clothed in the same jeans and tee shirt. Baby was sleeping and Sheena was nowhere to be found.

I peered into the lounge and at the clock on the wall—12:30 p.m. It was so hot that I shed my tee shirt and jeans, dropping them on the floor. Many of the other girls had done the same. We often sat around in our underwear as there was no point in getting hot and sweaty. I made myself an instant coffee by pouring into hot water a pre-mixed package including powdered milk and sugar. Returning to the lounge, I listened to pieces of conversations, all of which made some sense:

He's nice but doesn't live here … I don't mind "small" drinks, three of them are worth one Babycham … Dave is bolla, Shauna knew him too … it was taken from my locker and she had the key … I told him I was having my period … just ask for a loan … tell him your number's going to change, you'll call him … she wouldn't leave us alone without butting in.…

Baby appeared, looking tired. Her feet, like mine, were still sore and we sat swapping stories. In the middle of all of this, Sheena entered carrying two large plastic bags and wearing her usual big smile.

"Lunch is served," she announced, placing the bags on the small table in front of the television. She opened the bags and out poured mangoes, melons, papayas and various other fruits, along with three cartons of plain rice. We gasped, asking where they came from. She replied with only "your turn next time" and went to her bed to laze. One of the girls already had a knife and some paper plates from the kitchen. This was the first time we had worked the bar, the first time we all felt so tired. It was also the first time we enjoyed a fruit lunch but not the last. We found that there were many fruit stalls among the local market stalls all around our apartment area, and we soon learned to bargain for cheaper fruit.

We had had our fill of the sweet fruit and rice when Mimi appeared.

"These were waiting when I came home this morning," she said, waving a bunch of papers in her hand. "Your bills from the Philippines."

My heart sank a little. She continued, "I have added on the Hong Kong portion, the two hundred dollars I lent you all and so on, so here they are." With that, she proceeded to call out our names, handing a piece of folded paper to each girl as she stood up.

I looked at mine. Reading from the top: ... accommodation and food in Angeles, dance instruction, promotion fines, passport, exit visa, air ticket, transport to and from POEA, costume hire for POEA ... it seemed to go on and on. I read on down ... pick up at Hong Kong, taxi, costume, shirt, shoes and tights. I half closed my eyes as I read the total: 22,432 pesos.

22,432 pesos. The silence that had suddenly come over the whole room only indicated the shock of the final figure on our bills. I tried converting it to Hong Kong dollars. At just over three to one, that would mean some seven thousand Hong Kong dollars. I recalculated it two or three times, but the figure was the same. Seven thousand Hong Kong dollars, two months' wages. I looked up. The others were sitting there, stunned. Mimi was still standing. I am sure she had experienced this moment of shock before.

"Don't worry, it will be paid back slowly over the next two or three months." She returned to her room. Thoughts of the bar, the customers and the other degrading things disappeared into one thought. I was being done, trapped with no way out. I was going to have to work for the next two months simply to pay off my debt. Then I remembered that Mimi had told us our accommodation and food cost in Hong Kong was one thousand each month. Another quick calculation, and it was not two months but at least three. Five minutes ago, we were all laughing and talking about our first night, how many drink tickets we had got and the other experiences. Now we all sat stunned, clutching our debt sheets, and boiling with an anger we wished to hide from the rest.

The only place to be alone was the toilet. I slipped away and sat there for what must have been ten minutes. All I could see was that number on my bill and me dressed in my swimsuit. Sheena knocked on the door and called to me. "I'm all right," I replied. "Be out in a while."

How did I let myself get into this? Should I write and tell my father? If I did, what could he do? The only way to pay back the money was to stay in Hong Kong and work. A feeling of total despair came over me. I put my head in my hands and tried not to cry. I was trapped but there was nothing I could do about it. I flushed the toilet even though I had not used it, opened the door and walked out without even putting on a false smile.

Sheena was waiting. She put her arm around my shoulders and walked me to the bedroom. I listened to her as we sat on the bed but nothing she said made me feel any better. My bill was my problem.

Rose had arrived from the market. I could smell the food that she was starting to prepare. I knew that tonight I would be back in the bar—but with greater purpose. I was going to talk to everyone who came in and I was going to get a drink from every customer. I could do no more than that—work, dance, drink. Disgust was all I felt toward the promotion, the managers and the Hong Kong mamas. My only consolation, if you can call it that, was that I was not the only one who felt this way. I had a standard six-month contract with an option to extend it another six. After that Hong Kong immigration would insist we return home. If I could pay it off in three months, I would still have time to save some money and get out of here after six months. Yes, I would work as hard as I could to pay off this bill, save a little money and get back home where I belonged. I could do it. I *would* do it.

That night we ate in silence. We all had our own thoughts but they had one thing in common—a plan to get ourselves out of our messes. Little did we know that we were playing straight into the mamas' hands, just as the mamas knew we would.

* * *

Still dejected, I left the apartment with the others and waited for a taxi. I had already calculated that three hundred drinks bought for me would earn me enough commission to pay off the bill. We got twenty-five Hong Kong dollars for every drink a customer bought us. If we got him to buy the "special drink" at 220 dollars, we earned thirty-five dollars. The special drink was a Margarita, Babycham, or any other hard drink. When you consider a bar could buy a bottle of whiskey for less than the price of a normal ladies' drink, it was a profitable business to be in. It encouraged the mamas to keep pushing the customers to buy more drinks.

We arrived, signed in and changed, which left us a half-hour for makeup and hair preparation. This was to become our nightly ritual for many months to come.

Before seating ourselves around the bar, we glanced at the roster posted each night showing who danced with whom and in what sequence. If we were not dancing and no mama was present we had to watch the drinks, push customers to buy more, change ashtrays and clean the bar top—anything other than sit around looking bored. My new determination to make as much money as I could gave me courage.

Each time the front curtain was pulled open, all the girls would look across to see who had entered. This time it was four men. Immediately the mama moved in and the music was turned up. The first group of girls slipped off their shirts and took to the stage.

As the mama walked to the four men seated at the bar, I went over too. I wiped the bar in front of them with a cloth and repositioned the ashtray.

"Hi, what's your name?" I said, holding out my hand.

"Tony," he replied.

I sat and started talking. We had been instructed how to start up a conversation: *What's your name? Where are you from? How long have you been here? Where are you staying?* and so on. By then, we were told, we should have an idea of whether he was interested enough to buy a drink.

I even crossed my legs, intentionally letting the shirt slip open a little. *What the hell, I will do the same as the rest, get the customer interested, get some drinks off him, then if he asks me out, make an excuse.* I still felt I was in control and I could make this work. I had to make it work. I needed the money.

I could see Mimi was pleased when Tony offered me a drink without being asked. The other three men were talking away about football or something, but he was happy to talk to me. He offered me a cigarette. I said *no* but thanked him. I even took his lighter and lit his cigarette as I had seen others do the night before. He touched my hand to steady it as he drew on the flame. He thanked me and I passed the lighter back. I held his hand for a few seconds before toasting him with my drink.

It was my turn to dance. I took off my shirt and placed it on the stool, telling him, "I'll be back shortly." Up on the stage, I adjusted my costume around the bottom and between my legs. Just as the other girls did, a little show in itself. Did we really need two pairs of tights to keep us well hidden? At the end of each song, I would stand there pulling the costume up and down between my legs and around my bum, placing it neatly back in place. I looked at Tony as I did that, smiled, turned around and continued dancing. Tony looked to be in his mid-twenties. He had broad shoulders and strong arms. When I helped him with his cigarette I had noticed a roughness in his hands, which made me think he didn't work in an office.

I finished my session and returned to Tony. They had since ordered another beer. Before I sat down I took some tissue and wiped the sweat from my face and chest. I made sure he saw me before slipping on the shirt.

"Phew," I said. "It's hot up there." I drank and waited. Would he buy me another? His friends were still talking away and, though they watched the girls dance, did not show any real interest. He offered me another drink and I called Mimi. She smiled and brought one over, placing the 110 dollar drink voucher into the pot. "Cheers," I said, raising my glass again. I held his hand and we talked for a while, then his friends said they were going.

"You coming with us?" they asked him. He said he was and got out his wallet to pay. We were not allowed to handle the money. All we could do was give the pot with the money in it to the mama. She would get the change on a tray and offer it to the customer, always expecting and sometimes demanding a tip. The tips, which went into a box, the mamas shared. If the customer gave us girls a tip directly and the mamas saw this happen, it was assumed to be a tip for them and had to be handed over once the customer had left. On more than one occasion in the months to come, I would devise ways to get the tip from the customer without the mama seeing.

As Tony finished his drink I started wiping the bar and returned the beer mat to the pile under the bar. I thanked him again for the drink and he said he might come back later.

I sat down with the rest of the girls and stashed my drink tickets into my bag. I refreshed my makeup. Sheena was up on the stage and doing her best to get the attention of one guy sitting by himself, quietly sipping his drink. I thought about going over and trying my luck with him, but I did not want to step on Sheena's ground so I remained seated. I watched as Sheena went over to him after her dance. Eventually she got him talking and was rewarded with a drink. I occupied myself by looking across at the door every time the curtain parted. A new-found bravery, caused by the urgency to earn money, was bubbling inside me. Had I lost my inhibitions? I wanted more and more customers to come in so that I could get drinks from them.

As the evening wore on I found two more "victims", as I now referred to them. By about one o'clock I had six drink tickets and felt content. While I was dancing, Tony came back to the bar. I caught his eye and smiled. His walk was now wobbly and he obviously had had a few more beers since he left us. He sat down and one of the girls went over. He ordered a drink and lit a cigarette. She sat down but he was watching me. I gave her a smile that said *Hands off, he's mine*. She stayed, keeping him company until I had finished and could sit down, then she relinquished the stool and moved away.

"Hello again," I said, taking my position on the stool.

"I've been to some of the other bars," he said in a slurred voice. "You want a drink?"

Of course I accepted. I felt a little sorry for Tony when the 110 dollar ticket was slipped into the pot. He had already bought me two drinks. Then I thought about my own bill and realised that he was big enough to look after himself and probably had lots of money, so why feel sorry?

He was not really drinking much and his eyes were beginning to close. I had finished my drink and Mimi came over. She could see that he was ripe for the picking. This knack of getting the customer at the right time was a speciality of all the mamas.

"What about a drink for me?" she said. He looked at her in a startled manner and said *no* but she persisted with trick number two.

"I'll buy you a beer if you buy me a drink." He was weakening and probably did not even want a beer. In the end he gave in, then Mimi said, "One more for the girl?" He was too weak to resist. She placed the two drinks down and poured out his beer, leaving half in the bottle. Then as I saw the two 110 dollar tickets slide into the pot, I did feel sorry. Mama asked if he wanted to sit in the booth for a while. This I learned later was trick number three. Get them to the booth, then get the girl over and demand a drink for her. The mama would sit on one side, rubbing his private parts with her hands and get the girl to kiss his neck and rub his chest. Once in the booth there was every chance for two or more additional drinks.

All bars had a series of settees known simply as booths but some had one or two booths surrounded by large, potted palms or tropical shrubs. These more secluded places were usually located in the corner or at the back of the bar. Here was trick number four. A customer camped out in this area stood a far greater chance of getting aroused, and would even be willing to accommodate two or three girls. This meant drinks, drinks and drinks. If a mama could get a man into the "forest", she knew it meant substantial money. In exchange for these drinks a customer would be given greater liberties. The fact that the San Francisco Club was an older styled bar and did not have forests was a relief.

Tony was tired and said he was leaving. Mimi said it was still early and if he came into the booth she would buy him another drink and get a girl to massage him. I could see he was tempted, but after looking at his watch and trying to focus on the time, he said in a slower, lower voice, "Got to go, maybe next time."

Mimi realised she was not going anywhere with this. Temporarily defeated, she returned to the other side of the bar, leaving me with Tony. I was holding his hand and gently stroking it with the other.

"You should go home," I said. Indeed I did feel sorry for him. "It's late and you're drunk."

"I know, I know," he said, pulling himself to his feet. He pulled out his wallet and paid the bill. He looked at the drink vouchers in the pot, counting them, but I don't think it registered how much he had spent. He still looked puzzled when he got his change. Mama had slipped two of the ten dollar notes under her thumb while she held out the tray, yet another trick. As he picked up his change her thumb held onto the two other notes. "Tip for the mama," she said as she immediately withdrew the tray from his reach. He smiled, too drunk to care, and the tip was put into the box. He said he might pop in another day. He had not even finished the drink Mimi had bought. I watched him stagger out through the curtain.

Mimi picked up the half-full beer bottle. This beer would be used again, either on a customer too drunk to tell the difference between a full and a half-full bottle, or consumed by the mamas when the bar was almost closed.

It was our turn to work late and that meant five o'clock. One of the mamas asked if we wanted to eat. We were all hungry so she sent one of the Chinese ladies out to get some food from one of the local 24-hour stores. By the time most of the customers had disappeared there were only five girls left, so dancing became a question of basically taking it in turns. I noticed one or two customers sitting in the darkness of the booths. The mamas were still trying to get more drinks from them and pushing the girls to go out.

Eventually the bar emptied. The music was turned off and the silence was bliss. We changed and left the stale beer and cigarette smells behind to find a taxi, dragging our aching feet out into the cool night air. We would all sleep well this morning. I had put my drink tickets into my bag along with the ones I had received the night before, counting them all carefully. Then slowly I climbed up to my bunk and said goodnight even though it was morning. That was the last thing I remembered.

* * *

The days became a week and soon we had almost completed our first month. Sheena had already been out on her first bar fine. She was very forward with all the customers and her long legs and pleasant personality made her a favourite. The man she went out with had returned on several occasions, asking her to go out, then one night she just said "yes". I don't know if she felt this was going to be "Mr Right". Bubbling with curiosity, I asked her when I saw her the next day, "What was it like?" She simply said he was nice and kind, and then proceeded to talk for an hour about the hotel. She had never seen anything like it before. Pure luxury beyond what we could imagine. She told us she must have spent over half an hour in the shower having her first hot shower and plastering herself with the rich scented soaps and shampoo.

Baby was less fortunate. She always suffered from bad cramps just before and at the start of her period. She told Mimi, who showed no sympathy at all, telling her that all women have them and not to be silly. In the promotion, Arnie had been a little more understanding. He would let Baby sit out from the dance practice if she did not feel up to it. But here in Hong Kong we were expected to carry on as normal. I watched Baby once, in obvious pain, trying to talk to a customer. Even he could see that something was wrong but she excused herself, saying she must have eaten something bad. At a local drugstore we learned that you could get medicine for these pains, and Sheena and I bought some for Baby. It helped give her some relief from the pain. This was just another sign of the mamas' lack of concern for our feelings or medical welfare.

Tony did not show up again. Once or twice I did wonder why he had not come back. Was it me? Was it the bar? Later I again met one of his friends who told me he had been sent back to the U.S. on short notice. I did miss him in some ways and especially when compared with the first night that I was forced to spend in the booth.

One customer had been buying me drinks all night and he was getting drunk. Mimi had noticed this and got him into one of the booths. I was told to join him. The booth could seat four people. It was set back from the bar in semidarkness, offering more privacy.

I sat down beside him. Mimi and another mama sat on the other side. The mandatory drinks were ordered and the conversation turned to sex. Both mamas were rubbing him between the legs and getting him excited. Mimi undid a few buttons on his shirt, took my hand and slipped it inside. I could feel the hairs on his chest. I ran my hand slowly around and then, as instructed, I leaned over and kissed him on his neck. He responded by trying to kiss me on the lips. I pulled away, but with everything else going on and not much room to move, he eventually managed to find my lips and kissed me. I felt little except the taste of cigarettes. I let him kiss me, and then his hand reached down to my legs and slowly started to move upward. Instinctively, I grabbed his hand.

"What's wrong?" he asked, drawing the attention of Mimi and her friend. I was well prepared, having learned from the others. "I am having my period," I replied. He seemed disappointed and I saw anger in Mimi's eyes. They carried on playing with him but he removed his hand from my leg. It was then that I thought of Tony. He had been nice. If it had been him I might have let him touch me.

Over the past two weeks I had lost much of my shyness, but that night in the booth upset me. I did not mind showing off and dancing or even holding hands and drinking, but I wanted to keep away from more intimate things like kissing and touching. Sheena said I was silly and it was not something to worry about. It was all right for her; she was now into this relationship with her "boyfriend" as she called him, and he was spending a lot of money on her. Not every night, but when he did come into the bar they usually ended up going out.

I asked Sheena about how she felt when a stranger was touching her. She said that she pretended it was someone else. "Who?" I asked. She did not know because she had not met this mystery man. She just had this idea of what he would be like and that he was the one touching her. I had never been touched and could not imagine what it would be like to have a hand on your body and not be in control of it.

* * *

One afternoon Mimi announced that the other girls from our old group would be arriving in a few days. We were all pleased. We could imagine their excitement but we also knew the problems they would face, not least of which was the bill from the Philippines and the long hours in the bar.

A few days before the other girls arrived Baby went out for the first time with a customer who had asked her out many times. Sheena told her to do it because he looked nice, but Baby was not sure. When she did make up her mind, I think she thought he was in love with her and she with him. I watched them at the bar holding hands, cuddling a little and giving each other little kisses. The mamas did not mind us getting friendly with the customers as long as they could see results, which to them meant drinks and bar fines. Yet I could see Baby's nervousness. He held her hand as they walked through the curtain. The next day she told us he had been very sweet and nice to her. The funny thing was, he never came back to the bar. I wondered about that for a while. Was it because he had got what he wanted and now was in search of a new experience, or was it that he did not want to get involved with Baby? Did she show her feelings too soon and frighten him off? I know it hurt her for a while.

Mika and the others arrived about the time we received our first salary. They were placed in an apartment in our block so we would often see them. We told them all the rules and what the bar scene was all about.

I looked at my salary and again despair hit me. My 3,500 dollars ended up as 1,360 dollars. I had to pay one thousand for food and accommodation and of course the two hundred back to Mimi. They deducted 1,300 dollars as part payment to the promotion in the Philippines, and with the 360 dollar commission I earned from drinks, I was left with 1,360 dollars. Out of this I would have to pay the taxi fares and buy makeup. My makeup had run out and I was using Baby's. And I needed another pair of tights. We took it in turns to buy soap for washing clothes but there were also the monthly sanitary napkins and other necessities. This month I would not be able to send any money home. Sheena and Baby were in better spirits. Her one bar fine had earned Baby an extra thousand dollars. Sheena, on the other hand, had been out five times. Lucky her. She could pay off almost half her promotion bill and still send money home.

The ease with which money could be made was to become even more apparent when Mika joined us in the San Francisco Club. The abuse she had experienced in getting to Hong Kong had hardened her. She threw away her feelings and just worked for money. She is the only girl I have ever known to go out on a bar fine the very first night. After that it was whenever she could and with whomever she could. Of all the girls now in our bar, Sheena and Mika were the centre of attraction.

Both girls knew how to be sexy. To Sheena's credit, she knew there was more to attracting a man than caressing him. She would do simple things with her hair. She would grab her hair, bunch it and drape it over one breast. Parade around the stage to make the customer take notice of her back, her height and her slender build. Her favourite tactic was to wink at a customer then look away, and wait a brief moment before looking back at him. She most certainly found the customer looking back at her and she would reward him with a big smile. She would do splits on stage or straddle the pole or pretend she was hiding behind one of the shiny metal dancing poles. If Sheena wanted a customer to look at her, he did.

Mika sometimes placed a thin scarf around her buttocks and tied it at her hip. This drew attention to her firm bottom. I heard one half-drunk customer shout *rip it off!* and thought he might venture onto the stage to claim it for a souvenir. Mika used feminine hand gestures, particularly when she sat close to a customer. She extended her index fingers up over her head and made circular motions in sync with the music, while her shoulders gyrated slowly back and forth. The two girls would often join forces on stage. Few men could help but gulp when the two girls danced backwards and bumped into each other with their bottoms touching. Standing back to back, they feigned playing electric rock guitars or pretended to be engaged in a western shootout, drawing and firing imaginary guns in opposite directions.

Some nights I thought the customers would fight over which one, Sheena or Mika, they were going to take out. There was, however, one difference between them. Sheena put on a great show but was more careful about who she went out with, always looking for the right guy. For Mika, if they wanted to go out, she would oblige.

8. Bamboo

Bamboo is one of nature's most versatile materials. People eat it, use it as building material, shape it into furniture, use it as a support pole for carrying goods, even sharpen it into knives. Yet despite the vast usefulness of bamboo, it is freely abundant and the ability to obtain it so easily keeps it from attaining the stature of something truly precious such as a rare mineral or gemstone. Herein lies irony: that which is easily obtained—however useful—can never be valued highest.

WE SETTLED INTO our second month. I was still doing well with the drinks. Baby went out occasionally. Sheena would selectively pick those men she liked. Mika was getting worse than ever.

One day we all met up for lunch at McDonald's. It was then that Mika told us that she had missed her period. My first reaction was shock but it soon turned to nausea when she told us how Len had taken her virginity and how she had been forced to have two abortions. I could not get that picture of Len out of my mind and how he took advantage of such an innocent young girl. I could imagine that weird smirk when he had finished with her. It just made me sick.

Sheena asked her how late she was. It was only by a few days, but Mika told us that her period usually came the same day every month. The conversation turned to what would she do if she was pregnant. Should she tell the mama? None of us had any idea, not having experienced this before. At home, it might have been different as there would be someone who would know. The last two abortions that Mika went through were organised by Len. Here in Hong Kong, who could we turn to? Sheena said she would discreetly ask around.

We left the subject of pregnancy, hoping that Mika would be all right, and turned to our other favourite subject—money. I told the others that I needed almost three hundred drinks to pay off my debt.

"To do that in six months would be around fifty drinks each month," said Baby.

"In a month, it's ten every night," Sheena said.

I was only halfway there. On average I was getting five a night, sometimes more but often only one or two, and some days none. I tried to join in the fun but found it hard. Sheena said if I was to go out with a customer a few times I could pay off the debt very quickly. I have to admit I had already thought of that. It would be an easy way to get out of my financial problem, but I still wanted to choose the man and the time when I would give up my cherry. As we walked back to the apartment thoughts of my sister came back to me. She made a mistake but it was her choice. I wanted the same opportunity to choose.

When we got back the other girls told us that Mimi had left a message. The American navy was docking the next day and we would have to start work even earlier. As if I had not had enough bad news. This was the last thing I wanted to hear given that we were already working hard enough. Sheena, who never missed an opportunity, said that with all those sailors in town who had not seen a girl or had a drink for months, I had a great chance to get those extra drinks. I hoped she was right.

* * *

Before it got busy that night Mimi spoke to us about the navy.

"They will get drunk," she said, explaining that alcohol was not allowed on American ships, "so they will all drink a lot. Believe me. I've seen this before."

"Officers have more money," she said. She told us how to tell an ordinary seaman from an officer by his actions, his tattoos and his friends. This did not make much sense to me at the time, but after a while it did turn out to be reasonably true.

She warned us not to go back to the ship. "Most of them will ask you, but going back to the ship is not allowed. It takes too long by boat to get there, and when you're there you will just end up in trouble. Any girl found going back to the ship will be fined three thousand dollars." She said that she would be watching us even more closely than before, and if a sailor wanted to take us out he would have to pay the bar fine like anyone else. "There are plenty of short-time hotels around here," she added.

Pointing at her watch, she reminded us not to be late. "Remember we start at two o'clock."

That night I made one drink. I was feeling tired and dejected by the time we left the bar. Mimi had let us leave at two o'clock, saying that tomorrow would be a long day. Mika went out that night again. I thought to myself as she left the bar, how she might well be earning a lot of money, but at what cost to herself. Sheena tried to cheer me up while the taxi sped down King's Road.

"Just think," she said, placing her hand on my leg. "One of those handsome sailors might fall madly in love with you and take you away from all this."

I smiled. In my wildest dreams, would that come true? "Yes, there might be one for all of us," I said.

Sheena, and Baby to a lesser extent, had adapted to the bar life much better than I had. In our brief moments of freedom, during our lunches and occasional breakfasts, it was always me who wore the long face. Sheena had money left over from last month. She had bought new makeup, which she lent to me. I was nearly out of money. The daily cost of the taxi, our food out and even the one or two luxuries like an ice cream or pot noodles were eating up the little I had left. My debt was constantly on my mind. I tried hard to get drinks off the customers. The thought of going out had crossed my mind on more than one occasion. Thinking back, the mamas must have known that even the shy or reluctant girls would eventually give in and start going out on bar fines. You can see the money the other girls are making and the fact that their bills in the Philippines are paid and the remainder of their salary is theirs to spend or send back home. I fell asleep that night with my problems still buzzing in my head, along with the thought of tomorrow, the navy, another long night and who knows what else.

Rose was in the kitchen early that day. I could smell dinner cooking when I woke. Glancing at the newly found alarm clock, I could see that it was not even noon. Everything had been brought forward—the cooking, the eating, the washing of clothes, the getting ready. We all seemed to be in a rush.

* * *

Going to the bar that day felt strange. It was daylight and the journey appeared different. This was only the second time I had seen Lockhart Road in daylight and it brought back memories of our first visit there with Johnny, the Chinese driver. During the slow drive down through day traffic, we saw lots of sailors around and a good few others in white uniform with an "MP" armband. Mama told us they were the police who kept sailors out of trouble. As we entered the bar, a few girls were already on stage and the sailors crowded around the bar. I headed for the changing room followed by several loud whistles and howls.

We were hurried along and told to "get out there". I slipped my shirt on and followed the others. As I bent down to enter under the bar, I felt a smack on my backside. I turned and saw this large sailor smiling and saying something to me. I looked away. I had never been treated like this before, as though I was a spectacle, there just to please them. But thinking about the whole bar scene and why they are there, "to please them" is exactly correct.

As I took to the stage, I looked around. The bar was full and even the booths had been taken over. Drinks were everywhere and wherever you looked, eyes were glued to your body. My first instinct was to revert to my old trick of placing my family in my mind, blotting out the scene around me. But if they were going to make fun of me—*hey little lady, you'd look even cuter sitting on my lap, why don't you show us your boobs* —why should I not get something in return? The laughter, the sly comments and the finger pointing were getting to me. They were going to pay for this "entertainment".

I took a deep breath, stopped dancing for a second and said a short prayer. Then I looked straight at the guy who had slapped me on my behind and stared him right in the eyes. I danced over to where he was sitting and swayed provocatively, pushing my hair up and sliding my hands down the length of my body. I bent over, pulling the bra cup down a little as I had seen Sheena do. His friends slapped him on the back, telling him "he was in there" and to "save a bit for us". I added a few more gyrations to my dance moves.

You are going to buy me at least two drinks, I said to myself over and over while dancing in front of him. He could not take his eyes off me, nor could any of his buddies.

When my dance was finished, I went straight over to him, slipped on the shirt slowly so he could get a good look at me, sat down and said, "If you want me to sit here, you have got to buy me a drink." I stood as if leaving.

"No, no," he said. "Stay. I will buy you a drink."

Got you! I thought. I sat down again and started the "what's your name, where are you from" routine.

There were not enough girls to go around, which meant two or three sailors for every girl. One girl had four sailors around her in a booth. Each was trying to outdo the other. I finished my drink and demanded another. He hesitated, so I asked one of his friends instead.

"No, I'll get you one," he said, pushing away the friend who was already getting his wallet out. As my drink arrived I thought the least I could do was show him a little more attention than the rest of his friends so I held his hand and stroked his arm, saying how strong he was. Don't ask me where I got the courage to do all this.

Two drinks already and I had been in the bar for only one dance session. I noticed that most of the sailors would buy a round of drinks for themselves and pay cash. Those who had bought a drink for a girl had a pot in front of them and tonight there were a fair number of pots out. Some of the sailors were already beginning to show signs of drunkenness. "My turn to dance," I said as my name was called. "Be back." I gave him a little squeeze.

I went through the same routine, showing myself off to most of the bar but spending considerably more time in front of him. He was smiling, pleased with the attention. Two of his friends finished their drinks and left—three remained, in what had now become my group of customers. The mamas just rushed around getting the drinks and it was good to see them working hard for a change. They were still keeping an eye on us but every girl was fully occupied. Jack, my sailor friend, had told me they were in for four days, some seven thousand of them. Nevertheless, getting time ashore was limited since they were only allowed out on a rotation basis. Tomorrow he would be back on the ship, but he hoped to get one more day on shore before they sailed. I hoped so too. I wanted him to buy me more drinks.

When I finished dancing I returned to Jack, more determined than ever and with greater resolve and boldness.

"Why don't we sit down over there?" I gestured to an empty booth. While dancing I had noticed some others sitting with one or two sailors in booths, and from the number of drink vouchers in the pots, they were doing a lot better than me. Again, he hesitated. "Come on," I said, pinching the hairs on his arm. "It's more private and comfortable."

What the hell am I doing? I thought. But I had thrown away any thought of caution and intended to make the most of this.

"Just for half an hour." I carried on holding his hand and pleading with my eyes. He looked at his friends and from the expressions on their faces he got the approval he needed.

"Okay," he said.

I led all three of them over to the booth, making sure Mimi saw me. One of the mamas followed with pot in hand.

"Drink for the girl?" It was too late for them to refuse. "What about you, you want more beer?" she said in her half-Chinese, half-English voice.

"Go on, we will split it with you," said one of his companions. He nodded and the mama called out the order as she returned to the bar.

I let him put his arm around me, the first man to do so other than my father. He squeezed my waist as if he was trying to feel how fat or thin I was. I tried not to notice but I was aware of his hand being there. We talked, the drinks came over, we said *cheers* to each other and we drank. The voucher entered the pot. I smiled and sat back, trying to act relaxed. We went through the usual questions *(do you have a boyfriend, a husband, do you have a girlfriend, a wife)*. I touched his leg once or twice, only a little above the knee. He was buying the drinks after all. I tried to keep his friends involved, leaning over or touching the leg of the one sitting on the other side of me. They mentioned that they were on their way to Subic Bay and looking forward to it, asked if I knew about the bars there. I said I didn't know but had heard they were nice. One of them said he hoped the girls were as attractive as me. Smiling, I told him I was sure they were.

Jack was a little drunk and tried to kiss me. I turned my head so his kiss landed on my neck. I held my breath and pretended it was not happening. He moved his hand up to touch my breast. I tried to stop him. But I could not pull away from him as his friend was right next to me and there was no room to move. The touch itself did not feel like anything. I was not excited. Nobody, except maybe my sister when we cuddled to go to sleep, had ever touched my breasts. I don't know how to explain the feeling of somebody else touching your body, even though it was still covered by a swimsuit. When I touch myself taking a shower, brushing my hair or any other personal thing, I know it is my hand. I tell it what to do. It is under my control. This large male hand squeezing at my breast felt alien and unnatural because I was not in control of it. I would not look at him and yet his hand was still there. I could feel him squeezing me. What he got out of it I did not know. I was disgusted. His two friends could see this and suggested they leave us two at it. I excused myself, touching the other one on the leg.

"I have to dance soon," I said, "so you might as well sit here." I pulled Jack's hand away, saying I had to do my makeup before the next dance. I looked at his eyes. The beer was taking its toll on him. I slipped past his friend and disappeared into the changing room.

I stared at myself in the mirror. What was I thinking of? All the promises I'd made myself about not getting involved in this sort of thing and now I was going out of my way to encourage it. It was fine that he was buying me drinks and that meant money. If I worked the full year instead of just six months I could still pay back the debt and save something. Did I really want half-drunken sailors mauling me for a few dollars? Back outside, Jack was almost asleep. I signalled that I had to dance. His friends pointed at Jack and called me over.

"We have to take him back," they said. I breathed a sigh of relief. As I walked back to the bar, I told Mama they were leaving. She was there in a flash, holding the pot. Jack was the one who had bought me the drinks and he had all but passed out. His friends were trying to get him to pay and managed to get out his wallet. He did not have nearly enough Hong Kong dollars and they started to argue about the price of the bill.

"A hundred and ten for a drink!" one of them shouted. Mama nodded and pointed to the price list on the bar wall.

"Prices all there," she commanded. She stood waiting.

Jack had slumped down again on the sofa. His friends were still complaining when the military police came in. They went over to where the noise was and stood there. The men calmed down. If they got into trouble they would not be allowed off the ship again. Mama was still demanding payment. The MPs took Jack's wallet and pulled out some US dollars. They passed it to the waiting mama. "I'll get the change," she said, taking the money. Later I learned that they loved American dollars. It was just another way to rip them off, giving a bad exchange rate.

By now I was dancing. I felt a little sorry for Jack, but thought again of his hand squeezing my breast and decided it served him right. Eventually the mess was sorted out and the two friends half-dragged Jack from the bar, followed by the MPs. I decided to avoid the booths and not stray from the safety of the barstools again, not even for extra drinks.

Sailors left the bar, new ones took their place. It was a neverending stream of thirsty sailors. We could hardly keep up with the demand for drinks. Normally we had time to empty the ashtrays and wipe the bar, but not tonight. I sat with at least two other groups and by one o'clock I had accumulated quite a few tickets. Other than the incident with Jack, I felt good. Three more days of this and I would be turning a profit— so I thought.

* * *

Sailors exiting our bar would very likely head for one of the other go-go bars, and likewise, sailors coming to our bar would have left one of the other bars. We never really thought of the other bars as competition, simply different places where girls like us worked. Lockhart Road was filled with go-go bars but there were a few more traditional disco bars. I had never been to any of them but had heard others say they were mostly frequented by Filipino domestic helpers.

On Sunday, the statutory day off for the amahs, these places were packed. Even midweek, many of the bars were filled by those few lucky amahs who had evenings off. Their enjoyment was simple—socialising, dancing, lip-synching with songs. Although the amahs earned less than we did, I thought of them as being luckier in many respects. With the free time available to them, they could set their own schedules. We worked without a single day off.

The disco pubs also attracted the sailors. For them it was a chance to dance and chat up a girl without pressure from the mamas to buy drinks. The managers of disco pubs recognised this and charged sailors 100 dollars as an entrance fee. Our bars did not have an entrance fee and of course there was the added attraction of girls dancing in bathing suits. The downside for the customers were the expensive ladies' drinks.

* * *

About one o'clock, one of the mamas brought us hot noodles. The bar was still busy so we had to take turns to eat, dance and talk to the customers.

Sheena and Mika had both been to short-time hotels located nearby. Only a few hours later, the two of them reappeared, freshened up their makeup and went straight back to drinking and chatting. I don't know how they felt about all this but I could see money written all over their faces.

Other than one or two scuffles in the bar and the MPs being called in to sort it out, it was a relatively peaceful though busy night. I stayed behind the bar and rushed around emptying ashtrays, cleaning the bar and serving drinks. I also sat and talked to the customers, which I hoped would please the mamas. They were all busy trying to sell more drinks and short-time sessions with the girls—where the real money was. So by taking over the cleaning and serving of drinks, I hoped that Mama Mimi would feel I had done a good job. As the early morning dragged on the crowds thinned out, through drunkenness or lack of money. By three o'clock the bar was almost empty. My feet were sore and my eyes stinging from the smoke. Cigarette smoke was bad enough but cigar smoke was something else. I sat down and was drinking a glass of water as Sheena came up and told me that Mama had said we could get changed and go home. Baby was still sitting in one of the booths with a sailor, so she had to remain. I sighed with relief as I took off my costume, stuffed it into my bag and slipped into jeans.

In the taxi going home, Sheena showed me a US fifty dollar bill.

"Where did you get that?" I asked, feeling the banknote.

"The guy I went out with, he gave it to me," she said, hiding it away in her purse, then added, "He said he's coming back tomorrow if he can get off the ship." I had seen that look in her eyes before. She liked him. She thought that maybe this was her man.

"He told me I am special."

I said nothing.

"Really, he said he had never met anyone like me before."

Sheena always believed that "this guy" was the right one. I am sure she had this dream that she would one day fall in love, be swept off her feet, get married and live happily ever after. That, if you can call it so, was her only fault. She trusted her feelings far too often. I know she had been hurt by some of the men she let herself fall in love with, but for some reason she was always able to brush it off and start again, without outwardly showing she was upset.

The next few nights produced the same constant stream of noisy, thirsty sailors, all intent on getting a little bit of fun on the side as cheaply as possible, and of MPs called in to sort out the drunk or complaining customers.

I stayed behind the bar, even though on one occasion Mimi tried to pressure me to take over a booth. She did not give me too hard a time though. Perhaps it was because I was relieving the pressure of the mamas to serve drinks and keep the bar clean. Perhaps she believed me when I said I had my period. Sheena and Mika both went out at least three times and Baby once. It was like farming back in our province. When conditions were right the farmer planted an extra crop of rice, knowing it might not happen every year. Most of the girls were also making the most of the situation, taking in an "extra crop".

If anything, the navy visit served to put me in the spotlight. The mamas had seen me refusing though I had been asked out several times. When the navy left Mimi railed at me, telling me I was stupid and to look at the other girls.

"It will take you months to pay off your bill at the rate you're going," she said.

The mamas knew I was a virgin. They told me on more than one occasion that the rich Chinese or Japanese would pay a lot of money to take my cherry. They said I would have to lose it one day, so why not make some money out of it. I don't know about the girls in the other bars but I was the only virgin in our bar. I didn't need the mamas to remind me of my lack of money. I was living it every day when my friends bought nice things. My reaction to all this pressure was an even greater resolve not to go out even if it meant working the full year to pay off my debt.

It was a relief when the navy did leave. Our working hours returned to normal, giving us a chance to rest and get back to our old routine. We all made a lot of drink tickets, and for some, a substantial bit extra in bar fines.

* * *

A few days later, I was in a deep sleep when Sheena woke me up. I don't know how she did it but she was always the one up before the rest of us, even though we had all worked hard and late the night before. She passed me a letter from home and watched me open it, eager to hear my news.

None of us received letters that often and we would share our news. Upon reading the opening lines, my initial happiness turned to tears. My grandmother had died. The dear old lady who had helped me so much during my early years, who had always been there for me as I entered my teens, who never had a bad word to say to me, my protector from my father when I had been naughty, was no more. I passed the letter to Sheena and cried. Seeing her sweet face in my mind, I said a short prayer for her soul. For once even Sheena was lost for words. She just cuddled me and we cried together.

In the Philippines it is a tradition that if a family member or close friend dies, money is sent to the relative who has suffered the loss. But I had no money and payday was still a week away. I know Sheena would have lent it to me but she too was waiting to be paid. I had no choice but to ask Mimi. She had always said that the mamas would make us loans. When I asked her later that day, she seemed pleased but added that it would have to come out of my salary this month. Reluctantly I borrowed five hundred Hong Kong dollars. I used some of the money to send flowers and sent the rest—almost a thousand pesos—to my grandfather. I enclosed a short note telling him of my sorrow and how I wished I could be there at the funeral. Mimi was likely pleased that I was now even more in debt and in one of her nicer moods she allowed Sheena and Baby to go out with me to order flowers and transfer the money.

When I next danced in the bar I could not get the picture of my grandmother out of my mind. I could see her the day I left the province, her warm wrinkled face, that last hug and kiss, her admonition to "take care" and "don't forget to bring me back some chocolate".

Payday was exciting for the others. But for me, I was still only left with around fifteen hundred Hong Kong dollars even though I had done well with drinks and not incurred any fines. Sheena sent back three thousand, Baby one thousand and me just five hundred. I could see that Sheena was feeling a little sorry for me but I told her it was all right. Next month, I assured her, would be different. I knew something had to be done. Mika had already paid off her training bill. Sheena owed around a thousand. Baby still owed almost three thousand and I owed more than five thousand. During one of our meals, the question of a bar fine for my virginity came up as a quick and easy way to get out of my problem. On the way back to the apartment, we stopped off at Watson's drugstore. Sheena and the others bought some tights and makeup. I kept my money in my purse. Then Sheena took us to a camera shop. At last she had money enough to fulfil the promise she had made while at the promotion.

Sheena walked out of the shop smiling. The camera had cost eight hundred and fifty Hong Kong dollars, including the film and batteries. The first thing she did was to make us pose right outside the shop for a picture, after asking a passer-by to take the three of us together. Sheena gave us a copy a few days later. I had put on my best smile, but when I looked at the developed photo I saw only sadness. Baby bought herself a watch and proudly wore it as we walked back. She would buy a camera next month, she told us.

We were in our third month and all the girls except me were buying clothes, jewellery, watches and, like Sheena, cameras. I tried to put on a happy face and share in their wealth. One day Sheena gave me her old makeup, having bought new colours from the market. I took it and thanked her. Then Mimi gave me a fine for having a hole in my tights, which would have to be paid that month. But I could not afford to buy new ones or I would have no money left for taxis and food. Sheena came to my rescue once again and gave me a pair of hers. I knew I could not go on like this. It would take me a year to pay off the debt and I would still have no savings.

* * *

The constant pain in my heart caused by my debt was affecting me. I used to enjoy our meals together but now I found myself just picking at the food. Even Sheena noticed that I was losing weight. She joked that maybe I was pregnant and stopped teasing just short of me bursting into tears. All I had was their friendship and now even that seemed to be fading, just when I needed it the most.

A few days later I received another letter from home bringing worse news. My younger brother Eddie had polio and was in desperate need of medicine and treatment. I sat on the toilet crying. What could I do? I decided not to tell the others for I knew they all felt sorry for me already and I did not want any more sympathy. It was as if I was the only one in the group with problems even though I knew the others had problems themselves at home. I folded up the letter and hid it deep inside my bag.

That Sunday I sneaked out of the apartment early. I wanted to be by myself for a while and I wanted to go to church, something I had not done since arriving in Hong Kong. I had to pray to God and share some of my troubles with Him. I had to ask Him to look after my little brother. I had no idea where the church was so I asked a man selling newspapers at the end of the road. All he said to me was "Central". I remembered seeing the station for Central during our tour with Johnny, so I got a ticket for the MTR and followed the signs to the platform. Central was only seven stops away. I had a tightness in my stomach, for if I got lost, where would I go? When the train pulled into Causeway Bay three Filipinas got on, chatting in Tagalog. As the train jerked away and entered the tunnel I approached them and asked them if they knew where the church was in Central District. To my delight they were going there. I thanked God for putting those girls on the train.

We talked throughout the short journey. When they asked about my job, I said I was a maid just arrived in Hong Kong. We entered the church together but I took my place near the back. I knelt down and prayed, harder than I had ever prayed in my life. I did not even notice that the Mass had started. I prayed for everyone, especially my grandmother and my brother. I asked God what I should do to get out of this terrible situation. I don't know that He ever spoke to me and I don't know that I left with any answers but I did feel a calmness inside as I walked back to the MTR station.

Leaving the church, I followed the stream of people down the steep hill past the American Consulate and into the road in the main Central district. I passed through Chater Garden where all the Filipino maids were enjoying their day out. I was pleased with myself when I found my own way back to the MTR station.

When I returned I turned my attention to washing my clothes and writing a letter home. On my way to post it I ran into Sheena and Baby.

"Where have you been?" asked Sheena.

I made an excuse that I had to send something home and was off to post the letter. They seemed to accept that. Posting the letter in the box just outside Tai Koo Place, I immediately felt hungry and walked back up the road toward McDonald's.

I sat alone inside, watching the families with their children, young Chinese couples experimenting with love and even the Filipino maids enjoying their cheap but satisfying meal. I wondered if my life would ever be normal. I walked back slowly, knowing that Sheena and Baby would be full of questions for me. I delayed my return so that by the time I arrived back Rose was serving dinner. They did question me and I chose to say that I had been to phone my uncle back home. We seldom went off to do things on our own and Sheena did not look like she believed me. Soon after dinner, before more questions could be asked, I left them to take a quick shower.

* * *

The bar was quiet and so was I. On at least three occasions Sheena asked me if I was all right. "I'm fine," I kept telling her. But I was not fine.

Don't ask me whether it was seeing the extra money the girls made from going out with customers or the now desperate news from my family, the constant bullying from the mamas or my visit to church. But my mind was half made up. I would "go out" tonight. I had to—no other option was open to me.

The mamas had been going on and on at me for the last two months about going out, persuading me that I could solve all my problems by selling my virginity. They had shown me that the other girls could pay off their bills and have money left for themselves and to send home. They had made sure that I had seen all this and had kept on reminding me. I could see the new handbags, clothes, makeup, jewellery and all the other "nice" things that I too would like to have. Although half of my mind said "do it", the other half kept fighting. I reminded myself how I felt in the booth with the sailors, and the feeling of hands on me. I could not go through with it. Even my poor brother's face in my mind, not dying but possibly crippled, could not seem to force me to do what the other half of my mind was saying. No, I would drink and dance and work for the whole year if I had to. I would not go out. I made myself a vow that from now on I would use every talent I had, whether that was my dancing, good looks or even just being a woman, to wind men up, get them going and earn lots of drinks.

Thinking back now, it was quite ridiculous. Why should a man spend money on me when there were equally attractive girls in the bar who would go out with them? If I teased them, it would not be for long. Once they realised this they would be off to someone else. Nevertheless, at the time it seemed like a plan.

On my second dance set I saw a man smiling at me. I had not seen him come into the bar but there he was, looking and smiling. I smiled back and carried on with my dance. When I finished Mimi asked me to come over. I followed her directions, shook his hand and accepted a drink. His name was Jonathan. He was here on business and had, so Mimi told me, visited the bar on many occasions in the past. I held his hand and talked as I had done a number of times before. Mimi stayed with us. I noticed that she was not pushing him for drinks. That was a little strange but I put it down to the fact that she was tired after the navy visit or had made enough to ease up a little. Jonathan bought me another drink without any pressure. Then it was my turn to dance again. As I danced, I could see Mimi talking with Jonathan. He had bought her a drink and they were looking at me and talking. By the end of the dance Mimi had moved him into a booth.

I finished the dance and sat back inside the bar. Mimi came over and told me to join them. She whispered, "He's very nice and very rich."

I did all the buttons up on my shirt and went over. A drink was already waiting for me and Mimi was there encouraging him to relax and enjoy himself. He was drinking whiskey and coke and the pot of receipts was near full.

He put his arm around my shoulders. I could see Mimi had her hand down between his legs. Several thoughts flashed through my mind but all I could think about now was money. He had already bought me three drinks. I leaned forward and finished the fourth.

"I know you're a virgin," he suddenly said, "but I want to take you out."

It was then clear to me why Mimi had spent so much time with him. She was setting me up. I thought hard for an answer but stuttered. What could I really say with Mimi listening and his hand on my leg?

I placed my hand on top of his to stop it moving. Using my period as an excuse would not work. "I'm sorry, I don't want to go out," I said.

Mimi interrupted, calling me stupid and telling me, "You can't save it forever." Her anger was unrestrained. And in a way, I could understand it. He was a rich, regular customer who was willing to pay a lot of money for me with a large commission for Mimi.

"You can't keep it forever," she said again. "Isn't it better to lose it to someone nice?" she added, stroking Jonathan's chest.

"I'm just not ready yet."

I felt Jonathan's hand pull away from my leg. He looked at Mimi and said, "I thought you said you could arrange it. You told me she would come out."

Mimi glared at me, burning her eyes into mine. "Get my bill," he demanded. "You won't find me here again. There are plenty of other places."

Mimi gave me one long, hard look and got up with the pot in her hand.

"I am sorry," I said.

He did not answer.

After he left Mimi instructed me to go into the changing room. I knew I was in trouble. She came in after me, shouting at two of the other girls to get out, and then started. I listened to her words—*stupid, frightened, stuck up...* they went on and on. Then she told me that if I did not go out I would be sent back.

"I don't need girls here who will not work."

I tried to talk but she was furious. I thought she might strike me.

"It's as simple as that," she said, pointing at me. "If you don't go out, you have to go back."

"But—"

"No buts, you either go out or you're finished. I've put up with you long enough."

I managed to say a few words—"But I am still a virgin"—before she laid into me again.

"I don't care, you're here to work."

But was I not working by dancing and serving drinks?

"We were all virgins once, you know," she said sarcastically. "That man would have paid a lot of money for you, do you know that?"

I felt tears starting in my eyes.

"Don't you start crying now," she said, "after all the trouble you have caused tonight." I held back the tears as best I could. She pushed me in the back, saying, "Get yourself out into the bar and remember, you are here to work."

I slipped back into the bar and sat down. Sheena was busy with a customer and Baby was dancing. Although the bar was fairly busy there was nothing for me to do. Mimi arrived back and immediately went into a huddle with the other mamas. They kept looking around at me. I felt alone and lost. Baby finished her dance, came over to me and put her arm around me. "What's wrong?" The tears were starting again but I forced them back, saying I would tell her later. I busied myself by wiping the bar, not looking at Mimi or the others.

Sheena came over to us and said she was going out. We wished her luck and she disappeared. I got up to dance, trying to pretend nothing had happened. It was my night to leave early but in her spite and anger, Mimi made me stay until five o'clock. Baby, bless her, volunteered to stay as well. She knew I needed a friend that night.

On the way home we shared a taxi with two other girls so I did not tell her what had happened until we reached the apartment. Sitting on Sheena's bed, I relayed all that had happened. I could cry now without inviting Mimi's anger. Baby just listened, holding me in her arms. Then in a moment of true friendship she told me, "If you don't want to go out, next time I will go in your place."

I could not believe that she could be such a friend. She was very selective and did not really like going out, but here she was offering herself in my place. Neither of us considered the fact that it was the man who chooses who he wants or that I was the only virgin, and seemingly a better prize for the man. "Tell him you have your period, but say your friend, me, will go out in your place." It was then that I realised how close Baby and I had become. Sheena would always be our strength but she had adapted to the bar life and was busy making her fortune. She was always there for us but she was more a part of this environment than either one of us. I fell asleep that morning with nothing resolved and with Mimi to face later that very same day.

At some point I awoke half startled—it was the sound of rain coming down in torrents and bouncing off the glass of the bedroom window. I knelt on the bed and looked out, barely able to see anything across the road. Listening to the storm, I thought of my mother and a memory of my youth.

At the start of the rainy season every year, when the first rains came, my mother would take out her brown earthenware pot, cover it with white cloth and place it outside to catch the rain. Then the whole family would drink from this "holy" water. It was supposed to make our stomachs strong for the next dry season and cleanse our minds and bodies.

I pushed open the window to catch a few drops of the rain in my cupped hand. I licked the water and said a small prayer. I hoped this holy water would give me strength to face whatever I had to, and purify my mind from its pressures. It was an odd little ritual, but comforting.

* * *

Sheena was not there when we woke. Then while Baby, Mika and I were sitting in the lounge eating some fruit, she entered with a huge grin on her face.

She pulled off her tee shirt and stood there in just her bra and jeans.

"What do you think?" she said, pushing her chest out.

Thinking she had bought a new bra, I said it looked nice.

"No, not the bra, silly. *This*."

She slid the cup down on her right breast and revealed a small tattoo about the size of a five Hong Kong dollar piece. It was red and heart-shaped with a green outline.

"Good, isn't it?" she said, showing it off to all the girls. "This will get them going."

I was shocked. This was the first time I had seen a tattoo on a girl. Baby asked where she had had it done and how much it cost.

"One hundred and fifty," she said, taking a piece of watermelon.

Sheena would have made a wonderful businesswoman. This little tattoo would earn her a lot more money than it had cost. She would use it to entice stubborn customers into buying her a drink. Sometimes she would stand right in front of a customer and slowly reveal the little red heart, then quickly cover it up again. She had positioned it low enough on the breast so it would not show while she danced, but when she wanted to she could slide the bra down a little to display it without showing her nipple.

The men loved it and it was not long before other girls copied Sheena. Within a month there were small tattoos on various parts of the bodies of other girls. One girl had a small green snake on the left cheek of her backside that appeared to be sliding down her leg from under her panty line. What she thought was going to be daring did not really work out because her mandatory two pairs of tights blotted out most of the tattoo. She did not worry but simply had another one done—the same green snake climbing up over the top of her panty line. To me it seemed excessive but the customers certainly found it interesting and amusing.

Baby and I never went for a tattoo. Mika did, as I knew she would, once she had seen the customers' reaction to Sheena. She had her name placed just below the waistline of her panties, small red letters enclosed in a heart shape. On more that one occasion, when I was drinking with a customer, he would ask where my tattoo was. It was as if they expected all of us girls to have them.

With many of the girls trying to outdo each other with the tattoos, the mamas were delighted. What Sheena had devised as a novel idea became a bonus for the mamas. Their commission from the extra drinks pleased them no end. They knew that it was Sheena who had started it all but not once did any of them even thank her for the idea.

9. Mud Slide

The tribes of southern Philippines are known for building settlements on mountainous terrain. This practice helps ensure that homes will not be affected by rising river levels precipitated by the rainy season. In the event of unusually large amounts of rainfall, however, rivers will overflow and the rains will loosen the ground, creating fast-moving mudslides capable of toppling obstacles in their path. The unfortunate person pulled in rarely survives. Unlike water which holds a person up through natural buoyancy, mud buries the hapless by knocking them off their feet and suffocating them while they are struggling to set themselves free.

MONTHS BEFORE, when I was sitting on the bench outside our house and my father was mapping out my future, I had a vision of an impending storm. Now I had the same feeling. My grandmother had died, my brother had polio, I was in debt and Mimi was threatening to send me back. The events of the last month with the navy, the bad news from home and now Mimi's anger at me made me forget about another problem that was about to blow up into disaster—Mika.

About ten o'clock one morning I was awakened by one of the girls.

"Come quickly," she said, pulling at me as I struggled to wake up. She almost pulled me off the top bunk. "Quick," she urged. "It's Mika, come quick." I stepped down and saw that Sheena was still out. Baby had already been disturbed by the commotion. One or two of the others were stirring in their sleep but turned over. I pulled on jeans and a tee shirt. Baby did the same and we rushed out. In the other apartment, four girls were crowded around Mika's bed. I pushed my way through and saw her doubled up in pain. There was blood—a lot of blood on the bed. This was not a bad period but something worse.

I rubbed her forehead. She was burning with fever and I asked her what it was. In between the pain and her tears she told me she had had an abortion. Only later did I learn that she had got a name from one of the mamas.

Baby and I got her up to dress her but she could hardly stand. We pulled on her panties and packed two or three sanitary napkins around her, then wrapped her in a towel which had been hanging over the end of the bed. We had to carry her down the stairs. Every time she tried to walk she would flinch in pain, crying for us to stop. I left Baby to prop her up and ran to get a taxi. Panic took over and I ignored the people staring at this strange spectacle.

I leapt into a taxi and guided the driver to the front of the apartment. Baby slid Mika into the back seat. I had forgotten money! Another mad dash up to our apartment, then "hospital, hospital!" we urged the driver. He roared away and we sat there cradling Mika in our arms. She was white, covered in sweat and running a temperature.

As soon as we stopped, we jumped out and struggled to get inside. A Chinese nurse came up at once. She could see the blood that was on all of us. A nurse took Mika away in a wheelchair. As we watched her being pushed away, all we could do was clasp each other's hands and pray. Another nurse came back five minutes later and asked us to fill in a form. It was then that I realised neither Baby nor I knew Mika's family name, her age or anything else about her. We filled in what we could—the Hong Kong address, phone number, her gender, her first name.

When we asked the nurse how she was, all she said was Mika had lost a lot of blood but would be okay. Then she disappeared with the half-completed form, leaving us alone in the room once again. Baby said she was going to the bathroom to wash the blood from her hands. I waited and sat there and prayed. *Why had Mika not told us?* We had been so busy with the navy and all the other customers that we had forgotten her problem. Baby came back to the waiting room so I went to wash.

The washroom was empty. I stood there, my hands resting on the sink, looking at myself in the mirror. The smear of blood on my face triggered a forgotten memory. It was the memory of when I was fifteen and awoke to my first period. Noticing the blood, I rushed to tell my mother. She hugged me and took me outside to the back of our house. In the Philippines there is a tradition to mark the transition from childhood to womanhood. On the occasion of your first period you must jump from an elevated step to the ground three times and then stand up and sit down on each step. This helps ensure that all future periods would only last for three days. My mother took me inside and wiped some blood onto a wet cloth before smearing it on my face. Washing my face with my first blood would protect it from blotches and pockmarks later in life.

I shook myself to bring myself back into the present. Still standing in the washroom and looking at my reflection, I turned on the taps and washed the blood from my hands.

When I returned a policeman and a policewoman were waiting to question me. I introduced myself and we explained what we knew. They told us that hospitals by law had to report such incidents. What they wanted was to find out what had happened and where the so-called abortion had taken place.

"This happens a lot," the policewoman said.

But we were of little help. These things would have to wait until Mika had recovered. So they took note of our names and addresses and left. The doctor arrived some time later and told us she was stable and that we could see her. We walked into the room and could see Mika lying there, her eyes closed and two drip bags attached to her arms. She was so pale, and if it were not for the gentle rise and fall of her body under the blanket as she breathed, you would have thought she was dead.

We both held her hand for a few minutes. The doctor said she was very lucky. "If you had not got her here so quickly she would have died." We were in tears as we left the room. The nurse told us she would have to remain there for a few days and asked if they should contact anyone. We would deal with it, I said, though we didn't know who to tell.

When we got back Sheena was there and so was Mimi. Although Mimi was not Mika's mama, she had somehow got herself involved. The police had already been round to the apartment and the mamas had all denied knowing anything about the pregnancy or the abortion. They would, as expected, all stick together, and Mika was now on her own. Sheena already knew from the others what had happened and we explained how bad it had been. Mimi seemed more concerned with what might happen as a result of the police investigation than about Mika.

Mika started to recover over the next few days. Mimi allowed us to visit her and it was good to see her sitting up and smiling once again. We never told her how close she had come to death, not wanting her to feel obligated to us. Mika had told the police that she got the name of the "lady" from a person she had asked in the street, and as to the location of the room where the abortion took place, she had no idea. The mamas had visited her in hospital and told her what to say. Mika, now out of danger and well on her way to a full recovery, simply had to comply. She knew there was no way the mamas would take any blame for this. The mamas had said they would pay the medical bill though in reality this would be added to Mika's account. Although she had been taken to a local hospital, which was supposedly not as good as the private hospitals, I could not help noticing how clean and organised it was, unlike the horror stories my sister had told me about the hospital in Tarlac.

It was from this experience of Mika's, and later of Sheena's when she contracted some form of venereal disease, that I found out we girls were responsible for our own health. If that meant visiting doctors or going to a hospital, we paid for it ourselves. None of us talked much about the health risks and we were never given any medical checks, even after going out with customers. The mamas never provided or even talked to us about condoms or safe sex. To them we were pieces of meat. There for maybe a year with another shipment to follow. If anything happened to us there were always others ready to replace us. When it came to health, we were on our own.

I recall one day how Baby was suffering with a bad tooth. Mimi told her to take some pain relievers and get on with her work. By the time we persuaded Mimi to let us take her to the dentist, the tooth was so bad it had to be extracted and she spent a week on antibiotics to clear up the gum infection. The bill was over twelve hundred dollars, and more than she would earn from going out on one bar fine.

The whole event, though sad for Mika, for a while worked to my advantage, as Mimi seemed to have forgotten about me. I was spared her anger while Mika was in the hospital, but once she had returned Mimi started on me again. She fined Baby and me five hundred dollars each for going out without her permission. If we had come to her first she could have avoided all the problems with the police. We argued with her but she refused to budge. I believe she did this to put even more pressure on my finances. She knew I was struggling to pay off my debt and the more she kept me in debt the better chance she had of forcing me to go out. All of the mamas told their girls that if anything like this happened again we must inform them and they would deal with the problem. I was furious. We all knew that Mika had told the mamas, but once again they were pulling rank and putting everything back onto us.

Other than the fine, Mimi made a point of keeping me late in the bar every night. She picked on me, telling me in front of the other girls that I was lazy and that cleaning and wiping were all that I was good for. On two occasions she forced me to sit in a booth, knowing that the customers would try to fondle me. She kept the pressure up and my life became an endless stream of personal insults and pain.

Sheena and Baby tried to make light of it and cheer me up. Perhaps they thought I was silly to make such a fuss over my virginity. I asked Sheena from time to time, when the subject came up, if she really believed they could not force us to go out with the customers.

10. Barking Dogs

In a full bar male patrons would crowd the front row, occupying every barstool directly before the elevated dance stage. With several girls dancing at one time, the stage was cramped and we danced close to the edge. To see customers staring up at you was less unnerving than knowing they were within an arm's length of your feet.

Several times when I had stayed out late with my friends in the Philippines, I was forced to walk the dirt roads with little if any lighting. Many houses had dogs and these dogs might be found sleeping in the road or resting in the dark. Passing in front of each house sent a shiver through your body. Whereas some dogs were asleep or took no notice of you, others would suddenly appear out of the dark, yapping, snarling or snapping at your feet. It was mostly bravado. And even though I had never been bitten, I learned to fear these walks home.

I DO NOT KNOW if it was one particular thing—the events over the last few weeks, my grandmother's death, my brother's illness or my friends' ability to pay off their debts, buy new things and still send money home. Perhaps it was the letter that I received from home two days ago asking if I could send money for my brother's medicine, or my salary which I had received showing all the deductions and leaving me with next to nothing. After the deduction of my loan from Mimi, my five hundred fine, the partial repayment of my bill, plus my share of the electricity, I could not send even five hundred dollars home this month, and it was this month when they needed it the most. What was going to happen over the next few weeks was going to change my life.

With Mimi still being her nasty self to me, my morale was dropping. My energy was being drained by the endless mind game I was playing: "Do I" or "Don't I?" Sheena and Baby were trying to ease the pressures but they too knew there was little they could do. I felt like running away to free myself of all this. However, with no money and nowhere to go, I was stuck. I often cried myself to sleep staring aimlessly out of the bedroom window. Oh, how I missed my sister's warm caring cuddle.

A few nights later Mimi called me over to sit with a man who had already bought her two drinks. I had noticed them talking about me while I danced but I was used to that by now and took no notice. I sat down and went through the routine. His name was Ted and he was from San Francisco. He said he had chosen this bar because of its name. He seemed pleasant enough as we talked. He had large, thick arms and a slightly greying beard. He said he was in his early forties and here on business, "computer software", he added. Mimi left us for a while and returned when my drink was almost empty. He commented on how expensive the drinks were, but in a lighthearted way that seemed to imply he was not too worried about money.

During my next dance Mimi came over and sat with him, and again I could see them in deep conversation, occasionally glancing up at me. I carried on not showing that I sensed a plot was being hatched by Mimi to satisfy her greed and her hatred toward me. I had resisted all her attempts to force me to go out and I know she resented it. She felt she had the right to manipulate all the girls under her charge.

When I returned the conversation had changed. Instead of small talk about work, it was now about boyfriends and me being a virgin. I guess he did not believe Mimi and had to ask me himself. Had I known what this was leading up to, I could have told him I was not a virgin, which might have reduced his interest in me. As it was, with Mimi there, I had no chance to lie even if I had thought of it.

I could see his attitude change now that he knew I was really a virgin. He was getting very interested, and with Mimi pushing him along it was only a matter of time before he asked me out.

"No," I said. Mimi pulled me to one side on the pretext of getting him another beer. She stared me right in the eyes and put a vice grip on my arm.

Through clenched teeth she said, "If you do not go out this time you will be back in the Philippines before the end of the week." There were no more games in her eyes, only fury.

"I can't."

"You will."

Again the vice around my arm tightened. "Now get back there and be nice or else." She put back her false smile and led me back, placing the complimentary beer in front of him.

I could not think. Ted held my hand while talking but I could not hear what he was saying. I tried to smile then heard him say, "Don't worry, I will be gentle, there's no need to be afraid." The noise of the music and his soft voice ran through my mind. My heart began to pound. I looked over for Baby or Sheena but they were busy. Mimi still had her hand on me under the bar where he could not see.

"I don't know, I'm frightened," was all I could stutter. I could not even look him in the eyes. The next ten minutes were taken up with his gentle persuasion, Mimi's steadfast insistence and my subtle excuses. I was waiting for my name to be called to dance so I could get away, but when my turn arrived Mimi told one of the other girls to take my place. I looked at her. She smiled at me. I knew this time I was beaten.

Mimi leaned over and whispered in Tagalog, "Three thousand will nearly finish your bill. It's that or back to the Philippines, I promise." Her tone left me in no doubt that this time she meant it. I nodded, my head bent in defeat.

"Go and get changed," she said in a voice that would make Ted think we were discussing the weather. I slipped my hand out of his and went to the changing room.

I sat there, my mind in turmoil. Would Mimi really kick me out if I refused? That was my biggest fear. If I were sent back now, how would my family repay the debt? It was like playing cards with Mimi, and in her hands were all the high cards. I tried to convince myself that it would not be bad, to remember everything that Sheena and even Baby had told me, but I couldn't remember a thing. I closed my eyes and searched my mind to bring back pictures of my family and my life before all of this. I was still sitting there when Mimi came in.

"What do you think you're doing?" she screamed. "Get changed and get out there."

I stood up and started to slip out of my outfit.

"You are going out tonight even if I have to take you myself. Two minutes!" she screamed again as she slammed the door.

Mimi had me. I was trapped. It was as if this whole bar was one big cage and I stood fenced in behind bars of solid steel.

Ten minutes later I was leaving the bar, my hand held tightly in Ted's as if he sensed I wanted to run away. The old Chinese doorman smiled, again playing with one of his false teeth, a habit of his, and said goodnight as we stepped out. I slid into the taxi, feeling that the whole world was watching me. The short ride to the Hilton where he was staying felt like a nightmare. I could feel him tightly holding my hand, not talking but just holding me to let me know that he was there. He never attempted to touch me, unlike what Sheena told me about some of her customers who would wait until they got into the taxi and then start mauling her.

As he paid the driver a neatly dressed boy opened the taxi door on my side. I stepped out and waited. Ted came around and took my hand again. Yet another doorman was already opening the huge glass door and greeting us with a "good evening". I looked around as we walked slowly though the reception. Indeed Sheena was right. The hotel was a marvel and something that I had never seen before in my life. We entered the elevator and he pressed the twelfth floor button. The doors shut and I was alone with him for the first time. He squeezed my hand in an attempt to reassure me, still saying nothing. The doors opened and we walked to Room 1207. I will always remember that number, the shiny brass numbers mounted squarely on the rosewood door. He opened it and stood back for me to enter first. I took two steps in and stopped. I heard the door close behind me and then he switched on the lights. He put his hand gently on my waist and led me into the room.

What had I expected a modern hotel room to look like? I had heard the other girls say how nice the rooms were with the television, sofa, writing desk and even a refrigerator bar. For a brief moment I forgot what I was there for and looked around. It was so beautiful and clean. The bed had been turned down and there was a small purple orchid and chocolate on the crisp white pillow. The desk in the corner was neat but covered in papers. Then I returned to my situation and shivered.

"Is the air-con too cold?" he asked, slipping his jacket off and placing it over the back of the chair.

"No," I said.

"Come, sit here," he urged, tapping the side of the bed where he had seated himself. "Don't worry. I am not going to hurt you."

I sat down with my bag still slung from my shoulder. He placed his hand on my leg and said, "I know you are nervous but just relax." He took the bag from my shoulder, placed it on the table, then sat beside me again. He moved my hair away from my face and let it slip down over my back. "You are very pretty," he said and kissed my exposed neck. I closed my eyes and waited.

I did not know what to do or what to expect. My hands were sticky and my heart was trying to break through my ribs. I could feel his hand rubbing my legs and his lips touching my neck. I remained frozen. Perhaps sensing my fear, he offered me a drink. I asked for a fruit juice in order to get a moment away from him. He returned with the glass. I thanked him and immediately began sipping the drink. I don't remember what juice it was. He returned to cuddling me and then tried to kiss my lips but I turned away. I heard a little annoyance in his voice when he said, "You had better go and take a shower."

I placed the glass on the bedside table, picked up my bag and walked to the shower room. I knew from the other girls that a shower before sex was the expected thing. I closed the door and locked it, ignoring the beautiful marble and gold-plated fittings. I took off my clothes and folded the jeans and tee shirt, placing them over one of the rails where the towels were hanging. Naked, I faced the mirror and looked at myself, viewing my innocence for the last time. Though I felt like crying, I took a deep breath and turned on the shower.

The hot water spurted out and stung my body. I jumped back. Never having had a hot shower, I had assumed that the water would be cold. I played with the water taps and carefully tested the water. This time I stepped in and crouched down. Normally I would have still opted to use a small bucket or scoop to pour the water over my body, but there was none to be found here so I let the water flow through the shower and down over my hair and back. I must have washed myself three times while I tried to think. But I knew I could not stay there forever, even though I felt safe with the warm water running over me. I got out. The mirror had completely fogged. I flicked back my long black hair, rubbing the mirror with a towel so I could see myself. I brushed my hair slowly with the brush from my bag and looked long and hard at myself again. Before putting my white bra and panties back on, I thought about makeup but decided against it.

I unlocked the door and stepped back into the room. I did not look directly at him but I saw he was already in bed. I placed my makeup bag down on the floor and sat on the bed on the side away from him. Then I felt the bed move as he rolled over and put his arm around me.

"Come on," he said, "get into bed, you can't sit there all night." He pulled the sheets back from under where I was sitting. I lifted up my legs, swivelled around and got in, the wet towel still wrapped tightly around me. I pulled the sheets up to my chin and lay there, eyes tightly closed.

I could feel his hand under the covers touching my legs. He pulled gently at the towel, saying, "You can't leave this on, you'll catch a cold." I did not open my eyes but unhitched the towel and let it fall to the floor. His hands where searching everywhere, my stomach, my legs, and he was kissing me on the neck and shoulders. "Just relax," was all I could hear him saying. His hands moved up and over my bra, then he slipped his hand inside the bra, touching my breast. He felt me tighten up. "Just relax," he repeated. His hand was there inside my bra and playing with my breast. I had this tightness in my throat but I could not move. He moved his hand away, then down my stomach, slowly sliding under my panties. I moved back with a start as he felt the hair between my legs but I could not move any further up the bed. I squeezed my legs tight together. "Just relax," he said in a sterner voice and took his hands away.

He sat up a little and I could see his huge and hairy chest, "Take these off," he said, pulling a little at my bra and panties. I lay there, closed my eyes again and pulled the panties slowly down and off my legs. I sat up and unclipped the bra, letting it fall away but keeping my breasts hidden with both hands. I slid back down under the safety of the covers. Still sitting up, he had lit a cigarette. He tried to calm me, talking gently, saying he was not going to hurt me but if I struggled it would hurt.

"Just relax," he said. He put out his half-finished cigarette and moved over to me again.

I could feel the weight of his body pressing against me as he pushed himself closer and closer. I felt his lips against mine and opened my eyes. His large round face was pressed up against mine and he was forcing his tongue into my mouth. I turned my head away and he moved his face down my body until his mouth was on my now uncovered breast. He was sucking at my nipple and it hurt. I half pushed him and he stopped. Then he reached down under the covers and felt the pubic hairs. I kept my legs closed so tight my legs hurt. He pushed his hand between my legs and touched me. I felt a shiver of fear run all the way up my body. Instinctively I grabbed his hand with mine and tried to stop him.

"Please," I said, almost crying, "stop, I don't like it." He released me and moved away. I could see he was getting annoyed.

"Look," he said, "for the last time just relax and stop resisting me."

With that, he was back at me. I could feel his penis pushing hard against my side. Then he lifted himself and lay on top of me. His weight pushed the air out of my lungs, and as I opened my eyes briefly I could see his rounded stomach pressing down on mine. He was holding his penis, trying to push it between my legs, but I was still holding them tight together. He pushed his knee between my legs, forcing me to relax my grip. Then I could feel his hand or his penis—I don't know which—pushing against my vagina, trying to force its way inside. I don't know how, but I found the strength to push him away, partly by twisting my body. Before he could speak I said, "Sorry I'm sorry". Then he half grabbed me and I could see the anger in his eyes. I pulled the covers up over me again in an attempt to hide myself.

"The lights," I said. "Can't we turn off the lights?"

He knelt there in front of me with his penis erect. I had never seen one before, other than when I had caught my brother by accident in the shower, but never like this. It looked so big. I tried not to look at it but it was all I could see. I thought of him putting that inside me. He could see me looking but made no attempt to cover it up. "Look," he said, placing one hand hard on my shoulder. "I have paid ten thousand Hong Kong for you and whether you like it or not I am going to make love to you." The figure of ten thousand blurred my mind for a brief moment. Mimi had told me six thousand.

"If it takes all night," he continued, "I am going to do it."

Again he returned, pulled back the covers so that my full nakedness was in view to him. "Now don't be silly," he said. He started kissing my breasts, my stomach and even around my vagina. I closed my eyes and just lay there. I did not want to see what was happening.

I felt his weight again on top of me, then he pushed my legs apart. I felt his hand, then his finger inside me and I flinched. He was supporting his body by one hand placed behind my shoulder, with half his body pressed against me. The other hand was fiddling with his penis and my vagina. Every time he seemed about to enter me, it slipped out. Holding that large frame on one hand was tiring him. He gave up trying to support himself and lay with his full weight on me. I gasped for air. I kept feeling this pain as he tried and tried again, then I felt a rush of pain right up my back and into my brain, and it stayed there even as I arched my back trying to move away from it. He had finally penetrated me.

I clasped at the sheets and clenched my eyes together, pushing my head back into the pillow as he moved out and then deep into me again. I saw only blackness; there was no feeling of pleasure. Again, he pushed and again I cried out. The pain was intense, but with his weight on top I could do nothing but lie there. I could feel his hands massaging my breasts and his tongue kissing my nipples. He was murmuring something like "so soft, so smooth" and he was gasping for breath.

How long it lasted, one minute, five or ten—I couldn't tell, but the agony each time he plunged himself into me sent rivers of pain through my body. I opened my eyes briefly and could see his large, rounded stomach bashing down against my slim waist. The sweat from his efforts was running down his face and dripping onto me. I screamed for him to stop but he pushed harder and harder. I almost blacked out and could feel my silent tears running down my face and onto the pillow.

I could not feel my insides any longer. After the initial pain I became numb and I felt nothing. I could only hear his panting and see his eyes tightly closed and his teeth clenched together. His breathing got quicker and quicker and his fat stomach slapped against me. My whole body was being pushed down into the mattress. Then with three or four mighty pushes, he flopped down on top of me.

Still panting from his efforts, he lay there. I felt a wetness between my legs, his penis still deep inside. I tried to push him off but he was too heavy. At last he rolled off, and as he withdrew himself from me a sharp pain again ran through my body. The sheets were now crumpled in a heap at the end of the bed as he lay there on his back. I glanced at his penis, now not as large as before but with blood and white streaks of semen on it. I leapt from the bed, not stopping to pick up the towel, dived into the shower and vomited.

I looked into the mirror. My eyes were red though I couldn't remember crying. As I lifted my sweaty hair away from my forehead I noticed that both hands were cut from my fingernails clenching my hands so tightly. I saw a smudge of blood at the top of my legs and thought, "I must get clean."

As I turned on the shower, condensation and mist slowly blurred my reflection. Like a soft white cloud, my face disappeared into a thousand tiny water droplets. The steam from the water stung my face and I searched the mirror again. I ran a towel over the glass, but without the presence of mind to turn off the hissing shower jet the mist quickly reappeared. I rubbed again and stared. From the reflection came the images of three different but overlapping persons. My mother's smile said

"We love you and understand." My brother was saying "Thank you my sister." My grandmother was whispering "Don't worry, I am with you." She was smiling and that was just how I remembered her. Her wrinkled and greying eyes looked sad but her unending smile, reassuring. I rubbed again to get a better look but they disappeared and I was alone.

I stepped into the bath, pulled the shower curtain across and grabbed the soap. I washed every inch of my body. I even rubbed soap into my vagina. It stung from the small cuts that he had caused inside me. But I had to get him off me and out of my body. All I could envision was his penis deep inside me and his sperm now planted in my body. I had to get it out. I took more soap and rubbed away at my vagina. I angled the showerhead up against it. Though the hot water was stinging me, I let the water rush in and run slowly back down my legs. I watched the water, stained with my blood, now washing down the bath—my virginity flowing away with it, gone forever.

Eventually I turned off the shower and stepped out of the bath. I felt numb and still dirty but now all I wanted was to get away. I hadn't thought about pregnancy, condoms, disease or anything, until now. There had been too many other thoughts plaguing my mind. My clothes were outside so I wrapped another clean towel around me. He was sitting up in bed, smoking. I could see that he had used my original towel to wipe the blood and semen from himself and it lay on the floor beside the bed.

"Come and sit down for a minute," he said, flicking the ash into the ashtray.

"No, I have to go," I said, clasping the towel against me and looking for my underwear.

"But I have paid for you all night," he said, stubbing out the cigarette. "I told the mama that before we came out."

"I'm not doing it again," I screamed. "You touch me again and I will call the police." I don't know where I found the courage and strength to say this but I stood there staring at him. I might always remember that fat, hairy body forcing its way into me but I knew that he would not touch me again that night or any other night.

"Okay," he said, "okay, don't get upset, you go now."

I felt I had won a small victory.

"You go now and I won't give you a tip," he said, as if the temptation of money was going to change my mind. Mimi had already ripped me off with her figure of six thousand.

I gathered my clothes and went back to the bathroom. No way was I going to let him see even an inch of my body again. I felt strangely pleased with the outcome. I did not want him in the first place and I certainly would not take a tip from him. Dirty, yes I felt dirty. Anger, yes, both at him and at Mimi, but now I felt in control and he lay there—fat, old and helpless. Not only that, but Mimi could never have a go at me again.

As I came out of the bathroom he called me over. I kept a short distance away from him. "Here," he said, holding out a red hundred dollar note. "Take this for the taxi."

I grabbed it and walked away.

"I'll make it worth your while to stay the night," he said. I closed the door and heard the latch take hold.

Once outside, my mind cleared. I would never forget what had happened or how I felt, but I could no longer see his hairy face or fat body and could not smell his cigarettes as he tried to force his tongue into my mouth. *No*, the experience would always be there but he would not. I reached the ground floor. What do I do now? He had said I was paid for all night. I looked at the clock: 1:30 a.m. I passed through the door and the doorman asked if I wanted a taxi. I nodded and he stepped out into the road to wave one down.

Standing in the small semicircular driveway surrounded by all this opulence, I felt the rage against Mimi grow. Ted was out of my mind but Mimi was firmly there. She might still be able to manipulate me in the bar, but now that I was no longer a virgin she would hassle me no more. I would be worth the same as the others. The taxi arrived. The doorman dressed in his gold-braided coat said goodnight and closed the door behind me.

"Where to?" the driver asked.

For some reason my old Auntie flashed into my mind and I said, "Happy Valley."

I decided I needed family tonight, not Sheena or Baby but family. An auntie I had only seen in a photograph was the closest thing to family that I knew in Hong Kong. I fished around in my bag looking for the address, hoping that I had brought it with me. I found it and passed the paper to the driver. He slowed down and turned on the light to look at it. Nodding, he handed it back and drove on.

When we got there, I handed him the hundred that Ted had given me. I did not want that note with me any longer than necessary. He gave me my change and I stepped out.

I could see the horse-racing track lit by the streetlights and the apartments surrounding it in circular fashion. Many had interesting front designs which reminded me of a few photographs that I had seen while glancing through a European magazine. Indeed it was a part of Hong Kong I had never seen.

It was quiet. I could see Rose Court in front of me and I made for the door. I pressed the buzzer. It took two more presses before a voice came through the speaker.

"Who's there?"

I could tell it was a Filipino voice by the accent. "It's me, Mary."

"Who?"

"Mary, your cousin."

A few more mumbles, then the door clicked open and I entered. She held her finger to her mouth to indicate that I should be quiet. I followed her through the darkened apartment to what were her quarters.

"What's wrong?" she asked.

We sat on her bed and I explained in between my tears as best I could the events of that night. As I was talking I could not help but see my grandmother's eyes and smile on her face. They were so alike. When I had finished she asked me if I wanted to wash myself. I told her that I had done that three times over. She told me to lie down.

"You stay here tonight."

I suddenly felt I had come home again. She lay down next to me, running her hands along my hair. "I have to be up early," she said, "to take the two children to school. So you wait here until I get back." I nodded sleepily. "The master is away and Mama will leave for the office before eight so don't worry yourself. Just rest."

She wrapped her arms around me and I closed my eyes and was quickly asleep. That night I had a short dream. I went back to earlier days when life was full of simple but happy times. I dreamt of our village and of the endless summer days that begged not to be ignored. Some days I would play hide-and-seek. Some days when the little stream behind our house was running slowly, I would plunge in and splash around in the cool waters. When the rains came we children stripped off our clothes and took a shower with nature, running around in the puddles before they turned into miniature rivers. We would chase each other through the water throwing sticks, and find our way across rice paddies and sugar-cane fields, all the way down to the river that cut through the countryside. During the dry season we could wade across in water no higher than our knees. But in rainy season the waters would swell and turn into a torrent of white foam, carrying along trees and other debris. In my dream I was caught in those floodwaters and was floating quickly out to sea. Then I awoke and within moments the feeling of the dream was gone.

I did not hear Tina get up in the morning. Nor did I hear her return. When she nudged me it was afternoon, and I panicked, knowing that I should return before Mimi noticed I was missing, but Tina insisted I wait. She made me some tea and we sat there, while I related stories of home and how I had become caught up in all of this. She was so much like my grandmother. Tina was horrified to hear how the bar scene was run, but what could she do? After all, she was only a domestic helper, who herself knew that work and suffering often come together in an overseas job.

* * *

She accompanied me to the tram to make sure I got the one marked Shaukeiwan. "It will go all the way to Quarry Bay," she said, waving as it pulled away.

As the tram wobbled and bumped its way along the tracks, I observed it turn at the junction with Hennessy Road and I glanced to my left. In the distance I could see the start of the Wan Chai area and my mind jumped to fat Ted, mean Mimi and the whole degrading experience, not to mention the questions I would have to face from the others. Then some thirty minutes or so later I recognised the North Point MTR station.

I paid my fare at the exit and walked back to the apartment. Sheena and Baby were both waiting for me. For some reason they felt excitement and couldn't wait to ask me how it was. I still felt dirty and degraded but I simply said it was fine. They tried to push me to explain but I couldn't share any of that experience, much less embellish it. I wanted to push it as far away in my mind as possible.

Then Mimi entered. She smirked at me and stood looking for a while. "Now you can really work," she said.

I gave her a glare that would have stunned a lesser woman but did not answer her.

"And five hundred dollar fine for being late back," she added.

I felt a rage rise up inside me and almost made a move toward her. I wanted to pay her back for the ordeal she had put me through, but Sheena held me. Sheena sensed my anger. She could feel my blood racing and knew I wanted to get at Mimi. She held me, knowing that I had lost control and knowing that if she released me it would only cause me more pain. Mimi smirked again and turned away, no doubt to write my name in her fine book. Would I never get her off my back?

Still in a rage, I pulled away from Sheena. I followed Mimi into her room, not even knocking. "I want more money for last night," I said, not knowing where or how I found this courage to confront her.

"What!" she said, turning around.

"He told me he paid you ten thousand. You said it was six and he hurt me as well."

"Well, he is lying." She stepped toward me. "Three thousand for you and three thousand for the bar. You think you're worth more than the others?"

She put her hands on her hips. "That is how it's always been. Now get out."

She turned away. Her posture and voice told me there was no point in pursuing this, yet why should Ted lie? He knew nothing about how the girl would be paid so he had no reason to lie. He must have known how much he had paid. It was just another bonus for the mamas at my expense. I would get three thousand and they would share seven. I slammed the door behind me and went to my room. I was determined to somehow get my share back. But how? They were always in control.

* * *

During the remainder of my stay in Hong Kong I met Tina on five or six occasions. Most times it was when I took my lunch and she was out shopping in the market. But twice I managed to meet her on Sunday during her day off. We would go to Mass and then share a simple meal with some of her friends. She, of course, would tell them that I too was a maid. I was always glad to be in her company. Her eyes and gentleness did remind me of my grandmother, and after all, she was the closest thing I had to family in Hong Kong.

11. Mangoes, Ripe for the Plucking

Mangoes can be eaten while green and hard. Stripped of the tough green skin, they are sliced and sprinkled with rock salt, sometimes dipped in bagoong—then eaten. The sharp sour fruit is treated as a delicacy. Some will wait for the fruit to ripen. As it matures it takes on a different texture and flavour. The soft yellow skin is easily peeled and the golden flesh is revealed. This juicy, sweet flesh is eaten, cooked, dried and turned into a multitude of other delights.

Mangoes that grow in the wild will grow to size, turning from green to yellow. Then they will just hang from the tree, bursting with juice, as if begging to be picked.

I SHRUGGED OFF the inevitable questions for the next few days, saying that I did not enjoy it but I was all right. The girls kept asking me if I would go out again. I guess they thought that now I had lost my cherry I was just like the rest. I played along to stop their questions, saying that if I did I would choose the person I did or did not go out with. This seemed to satisfy Sheena and Baby and they stopped asking questions. I slipped back into the bar scene with an even greater awareness of how powerful the mamas really were.

Over the next few days I made a point of trying to be a little friendlier to Mimi, even admitting to her, in a lie, that I had been silly to worry about losing my virginity. I decided to go along with her but made the point that from now on I would say if I wanted to go out. This seemed to quiet her down and she did not push me as much. I knew in the back of my mind that it would be only a matter of time before she started again. After all, the more times she could get me out, the more money there was for her. This was the best way—leave it open, don't refuse to go out, but insist that it would be my choice. In myself, I felt stronger now.

Although I had been able to stop the questions from Sheena and Baby and put Mimi on hold, I still felt bad inside. It was as if I was pretending to be happy for them, and even though I went through the daily routines and evenings in the bar as if nothing was wrong, my mind was still hurt. The more I tried to get Ted and that whole night out of my mind, the more it would reappear. I even found myself looking at men in the bar and hating them just for being there. Over the next few weeks I found I needed to be by myself, alone with my thoughts and away from the girls in the apartment.

Not every day but when I did feel really low, I would make an excuse to Sheena and Baby, saying I was meeting my Auntie Tina. I would walk up King's Road to a small park. Many Chinese people went there to sit and pass the time. It was not a large space but there were flowerbeds and trees with seats in the shade running along the sides of the paths. Even though you could hear the traffic rushing past, being in the park seemed to offer a little peace. I would buy myself something to eat and drink at the 7-Eleven store on my way and find a quiet spot to sit.

One day, while I was sitting there watching the world go by and eating my sandwich, I saw Mika on a bench at the far side of the park. I was about to get up and go over to her when I saw a man sit down next to her. By the way they were talking, he was not a stranger. I watched for what must have been only a few minutes and then they got up together and walked slowly out of the park. I knew she had not seen me and the way she was acting with the man I could guess what she was up to. Then the thought of her illegal abortion jumped into my mind and I wondered if she was in trouble again. I stood up looking for them, half thinking that I would go after her to see that she was all right, but they were not in sight.

That night in the bar, I asked her how she was and she said "fine". But the incident in the park was still on my mind. I had not said anything to the others and maybe I was worrying too much, but with everything that Mika had endured in the past, I just wanted to be there for her. During one of our non-dancing breaks I asked her to come to the changing room with me. Fortunately the room was empty. I told her what I had seen that morning and added that I had not told any of the others. She made me swear that I would never tell anyone, then she relayed the whole story.

145

A few months back one of her more regular Chinese customers took her out for the night. He was married, so they went to one of the short-time hotels. These hotels rented rooms by the hour with no need to register or for I.D. cards. He suggested they meet during the daytime, during his lunch break. That way he could avoid the very expensive bar fine and pay Mika cash for a short time in a hotel. At first I felt disgusted, but then knowing Mika was only in this for the money, and after she had assured me she was happy with the arrangement and that he was always nice to her, I felt glad that for once the mamas were losing out. She told me that two or three times each month they would meet at the Victoria Villa Hotel and he would give her five hundred Hong Kong dollars every time. Because they always met each other around one o'clock, she could be back in the apartment and ready for work without anyone knowing she had been out. For all they knew she had been out for lunch. She swore me to secrecy once again and said I should consider doing the same as it was such easy money. Then she gave me a short embrace and returned to the bar.

* * *

One evening when the bar was quiet Mimi came up and spoke to me in a very low and calm voice, using a tone I had not heard before. She said that even though I had been out once there was still a lot of money to be made.

"We can still say you're a virgin," she said. "The customer will not know, and let's face it, you are still going to be a little shy and nervous."

I could see her mind working away—another easy seven thousand for her. I told her I would think about it. When she had returned to the others, I thought about it. If I went along with her and then told the man the truth when we got to the hotel, he would be annoyed. He would have paid a fortune and not got a virgin. He might even storm back to the bar and take it out on Mimi. This indeed was worth thinking about.

I talked to Sheena about my idea over lunch. She was shocked that I would even consider it. "She will kill you," she said. "You know the bars have Triad connections. They could do anything they wanted with you and nobody would know." This frightened me and so I thought about it for some time. Mimi would take it out on me forever and my life would be a living nightmare. I put the idea of revenge out of my mind. I hated being manipulated. I hated the bars, the customers and most of all Mimi. However, I knew there was nothing I could do. I had seen the mamas' total lack of concern for us through Mika's abortion, even Baby's tooth problem. To them we were just a means to make money and they would use us to that end until our contract was finished.

Yet they would expect me to go out again and I wanted at least to be in control of it. So the following night I told Mimi in the bar that I would go along with her, pretending to be a virgin, but that I would choose the customer and get five thousand for it, not three. She agreed.

I even felt a sense of relief that with the five thousand I would have found a way to pay off my bill and have some money left over.

A week or so later Mimi did her work on a Japanese guy who was obviously rich and a bit drunk. I went through all the preliminaries at the bar and even spent a session in the booth with Mimi and him before he agreed to pay the bar fine. I did not have to pretend I was frightened. I was. Thoughts of not just the pain but also the embarrassment of showing my body to a complete stranger were still in my mind. Memories of Ted massaging and touching me came back and I felt dirty again before we had even reached the hotel. He was staying at the Mandarin.

I followed him to his room and he immediately sat on the bed and took off his shirt. "Not fat like Ted," I thought, relieved. I signalled at the shower. He nodded and lit up a cigarette.

This time I knew what to expect. I returned with the towel around me and sat next to him. He put his arm around me and I flinched.

"Rerax," he said in his Japanese accent. *Was this the only thing men said to women before sex?* He removed the towel. I covered my breasts even though I still had my bra on. He said something in Japanese and then started kissing me.

I lay there looking up at the ceiling, feeling his hands all over my body. I could only compare the situation with my one experience with

Ted, who had me naked in less than a few minutes. This Japanese guy seemed to want me to keep my panties on. He kept rubbing my vagina through my panties. Sheena told me later that most Japanese are like this, but at the time I thought it strange. I was still tense and resisting him and he kept mumbling things in Japanese. Eventually he pulled my panties down and tried to kiss me there. I pushed him away, saying *no*. He stopped and removed his trousers and briefs. He lay down and started to kiss me. I could taste the cigarette on his breath and closed my eyes. He angled himself on top of me and, still mumbling, started to work his finger inside me. He forced my legs apart and found my vagina. He rubbed furiously up and down until it became a little wet. Sheena said she liked the man to play with her first as it felt good, but I felt nothing other than embarrassment. Then he was fully on top of me and pushing to get inside.

The rush of pain again ran through me as he forced himself in. I gasped a little as he squeezed my breast, still in my bra. The pain was not quite as bad as before but it still hurt every time he moved up and down on me, grunting. He fumbled with my bra, trying to remove it, yet not wanting to stop his rhythm. In the end he pulled it down to expose my breasts and there it remained, my bra wrapped around my waist.

He sat up and pushed down on my legs now spread wide. He was pushing against my knees and it hurt. I tried to move but could not. He pushed and pushed, faster and faster, then, just as I opened my eyes, he stopped. His face was contorted as if he was in pain. He took himself out of me and held his penis in his hand. His eyes were firmly closed as he ran his hand up and down his penis, quicker and quicker. I saw a little blood on it. He gasped. Then he released his hand and his semen shot out all over my body. Having fully ejaculated, he lay back on top of me, squashing his semen between us.

I felt dirty and degraded. The girls talked of their experiences but I had never heard of this. Still panting, he at last rolled over. The semen he had squashed between us was sticking to our skin. I got up, grabbed the towel and made for the shower.

I went through the cleaning ritual, still not fully believing what I had seen: the semen shooting from his penis, his face squeezed tightly in pain. I did not want to touch the sticky white stuff with my hands and used the shower to flush it off my body. I dressed completely but not before wiping off my bra with a face towel. I was not going to give him a chance to ask me to stay. Before leaving the bathroom I stuffed the small bottles of shampoo, conditioner and body lotion that the hotel provided for their guests into my bag. I had heard the others talk about their collection from the different hotels. I did not intend to start such a collection but rather enjoyed a small feeling of satisfaction in doing this.

When I returned to the room, he was sitting on the bed, smiling hugely, another cigarette in his hand. He thought he had just taken my cherry and I knew that I had cheated him. As I sat on the side of the bed putting on my shoes, I made a bet with myself that he would go home to his friends and boast how he took the cherry of the beautiful Filipina.

"You velly nice girl," he said as I stood up. "I come see you again."

Then he reached over for his wallet, took out two hundred American dollars and gave it to me. I tried to work out how much it was worth in pesos.

"Thank you," he said. "You go now." I let him kiss me on the cheek then simply said goodnight and left him to his dreams.

It was only two o'clock as I left the hotel. I gave the doorman a five Hong Kong dollar tip, told the taxi driver where to go and sat back. I had mixed feelings. I still felt bad about the whole thing, especially after being sprayed with his semen, but I was holding two hundred dollars and I knew Mimi would not be able to manipulate me any more. Even better, she would never know about the money tucked safely in my purse. As we headed back toward Wan Chai, I calculated that it was over four thousand pesos. It was for sure the most money I had ever held in my hand.

When I reentered the bar, Sheena, who was on the stage, gave me a smile that said *Are you okay?* I smiled back. Mimi came over before I got to the changing room and said, "Don't worry about getting changed, you can go home if you want."

The bar was not busy so I thanked her and sat down to wait for Sheena. Maybe she thought that now she had won and could use me as she wanted. Little did she know that I was now in control and she could not pressure me or hurt me any more.

Twenty minutes later we were in a taxi heading home. I told Sheena about what the Japanese man had done. She pulled a face of disgust. They are funny like that, she said. I showed her the two hundred American dollars and she gave me a squeeze.

"Great, let's change it and have lunch tomorrow."

The rest of the month drifted by quickly. I did not go out any more that month and Mimi had now almost given up with her pressure tactics. The Japanese guy did return two nights later, with two of his friends. He was talking away, no doubt about what a man he was and how he had taken my cherry. Thankfully he never bought a drink or even suggested going out. They just sat there for over an hour, staring. He would point and they would laugh. I felt humiliated. If I had no money in the world and was completely desperate, I would never let him see me naked again.

My period arrived a few days after my night out with the Japanese guy. I had indeed washed all of Ted's semen out of myself and the nagging thought that had bothered me was put to rest. If I had been pregnant, what would I have done? I don't think I could have been like Mika and had an abortion, that was just not part of my upbringing. I remember one day slipping away to the park and thinking about it. I did not want to be pregnant and certainly not from Ted. How stupid I had been not to make him use a condom. This silly mistake could have completely ruined my life. I could see myself pregnant and having to return home with nothing except a future of poverty and a child who would never know its father. So that morning, when I awoke to my period, I said several prayers of thanks and determined never to put myself at risk again.

My salary came, and even after paying my fine I had enough to pay my bill off in full and to send home more than six thousand pesos. I knew they would be pleased. It still hurt me that Mimi had ripped me off of Ted's bar fine, but I was pleased that I had got a full five thousand for the

Japanese guy. From now on I would be on the same commission as the rest of the girls, one thousand for each bar fine. The mamas took the other two thousand five hundred. I often thought about how much value should be placed on a virgin. Should it be measured in money? But it was too late for me. Thinking about it would only bring back the hate I had for Mimi, so I resigned myself to what had happened and tried to forget it.

I kept some money for myself, bought makeup and some nice underwear. When no one was looking, I threw away the panties I had worn when I went out with Ted. Every time I put them on it reminded me of that terrible night. I had been used and had to accept it. But even with all these bad memories, I had been able to resolve two of my biggest problems. I had paid off my debt and Mimi could no longer push me around. I am not saying it was worth it, but looking back I know I would only have been able to hold out against the pressure for so long.

Most of the girls I talked to who were virgins when they came to Hong Kong said the same thing. The pressure for money from home and the pressure from the mamas to force you out by keeping you poor eventually become intolerable. The lifestyle that you see so many of the other girls develop, including the things they buy, is always there staring you in the face. You know you can have the same if you're prepared to give up your cherry. The whole bar scene is a recipe that catches you no matter how strong you think you are.

We entered a new month and two Australian navy ships arrived. I noticed that, unlike with the Americans, few short-time bar fines took place. The sailors were far more interested in their beer and spent hours looking at the girls. Drink tickets were few and far between and no matter how hard we pushed, they nearly always said no. The mamas knew this, ignored them and left the sailors to us girls. During the navy tours, regular customers would usually stay away. I asked one man why this was and he told me that it was too crowded and there was always trouble. "It's easier to wait till they have gone," one customer said. "You girls will still be here."

A few weeks later my cousin Roseanna arrived to start work as a dancer. She was staying in another apartment, but being my blood cousin she was soon accepted into our little group. She was dancing in the Hawaii Club, a little way down and across the street from our bar. I spent a lot of time with Roseanna, explaining what went on and what to be careful about. She was not a virgin and had a steady Filipino boyfriend of almost a year. But the inevitable money shortage in the family caused her to come to Hong Kong. I think my father had something to do with this, as most of my letters home tended to bring out the good things. I would hardly tell my parents in my letters that all I wanted to do was come home.

The vast majority of girls working in the Wan Chai go-go bars were Filipina but a handful of bars had a few Thai working as well. The Hawaii Club was an exception. It had been an entirely Thai bar, including its Thai mamasans. Roseanna would be one of two Filipinas to start working there. Some people said that a couple of Wan Chai bars had experimented in the past with a 50-50 mix of Filipino and Thai girls but had found that quarrels among the girls became commonplace. I imagine that this was due to language. Because Thai girls spoke very little English and Filipinas spoke no Thai, living and working together would wear the girls down and lack of communication would result in squabbles. Customers who sought to chat up a bar girl enjoyed Filipinas more. Some customers did prefer Thai girls. Perhaps they were more exotic than we were. I had also heard that mamasans at Hawaii Club were considerably less pushy when it came to getting customers to buy drinks. Some customers responded with more frequent visits.

* * *

One night we were going through our routines, dancing, drinking and trying to chat up the customers, but little was happening. The last few days had been a quiet spell. Then a man came in. We all looked across as usual, as none of us had seen him before. Sheena had just finished dancing and slid across the bar to sit next to him.

152

"What do you want to drink?" she asked, placing the beer mat in front of him.

"Beer," he said. "Carlsberg."

Sheena sat with him and waited for his drink to arrive. She put on her shirt and started to talk. I was dancing by then and watched her rubbing his arm and asking for a drink. After she had shown him her tattoo a few times he gave in and her drink arrived. Sheena and her beauty were a challenge for any man. She smiled at me as she took a sip and went back to her conversation. When I saw Mimi arrive at their side, I knew he was interested and this was confirmed a few drinks later when Sheena got up to change.

That night, as Sheena left the bar arm in arm with her new companion, we all made the normal comments in Pampangan, *mimingat ka ne siguro iyan na ing totung lalaki para keka*—be careful with him, and maybe this time he will be the right one for you. We never thought that by the end of the night she would be in a mess. He had bought her three or four drinks and had watched her dance with obvious pleasure. He did not argue about the price of the bar fine as many customers would, but paid in cash straight to Mama. Sheena left to get changed and he watched her disappear into the changing room before returning to his drink. He looked perfectly normal, just another lonely businessman who wanted company for the night. She turned and waved at us as he lifted the curtain for her to leave. What happened next was a shock and warning to us all.

They chatted in the taxi as they drove back to the hotel. Once inside he offered her a drink, pouring himself a beer from the mini bar. He passed her the fruit juice that she asked for and he kissed her gently on the lips as they sat on the edge of the bed. He sipped his beer and they talked and kissed for a while longer. Sheena told us she felt him and he was excited, so she stood up and said she would take a shower. When she returned he was already in the bed with the covers pulled up above his waist. She slipped off the towel wrapped around her body and sat to one side. She had put her bra and panties back on.

"They prefer that," she used to say. "It gets them more excited wh[...] they see you and know they have to remove them."

He caressed her arms and shoulders and pulled back the sheets [...] her to get in. She slipped herself between the sheets and pressed hers[...] against him. Kissing him gently, she moved down his body until she cou[...] feel his penis against her face. Then she felt his hand grab her by the ha[...] At first she took no notice, but he pulled at her. He was being rough a[...] she assumed he did not want her to kiss him there, so she moved ba[...] up his body. He slipped her bra off and fumbled to remove her panti[...] She obliged by pushing them down one leg with her other foot. He roll[...] her over onto her back and sat astride, pinning her arms down on t[...] pillow. His face was red and he had a strange glare in his eyes. He ma[...] no attempt to be gentle, rather thrusting himself against her in an eff[...] to penetrate. Sheena gasped and told him to be gentle.

"Shut up, you slag," was his reply and he struck her across the fa[...] She winced in pain as he pinned her down again. Her wrists were hurti[...] her face smarting from the blow, and still he pushed and pushed.

She struggled to free her hands, twisting her head from side to si[...] Then he finally managed to push himself inside her. For a moment s[...] stopped her struggle as the pain inside her caused her to draw her brea[...] She shouted at him to stop, but he slapped her again, telling her to ke[...] quiet. Again she screamed. He placed a hand over her mouth. She tri[...] to bite but he squeezed her jaw until she thought it would break. Wi[...] her free hand she tried to push him away, scratching his face. He slapp[...] her again. Tears were rolling down her cheeks as she lay there helple[...] She closed her eyes and remained motionless, trying not to feel wh[...] was happening. Then she could hear him panting and she felt he wou[...] finish soon. Instead, he withdrew from her and turned her over. Grabbi[...] her hair in one hand, with the other he pinned her shoulders to the be[...] Then he forced himself into her anus. The pain was so intense she thoug[...] she would pass out. She could not scream as her face was buried in t[...] pillow. She could feel her insides tearing as he pushed and pushed hims[...] deep into her. Then he gasped and flopped down on top of her, his weig[...]

squeezing the last air from her lungs, so she too gasped for air through the suffocating pillow. He slowly withdrew from her and rolled over, panting.

She did not know what to do—run, scream for help or just hope he would tell her to go. Without looking at him, she edged to the side of the bed, until he again grabbed her hair and pulled her back. She held the hand pulling at her hair to relieve the pain.

"Where are you going?" he screamed into her bent-back face. "I've paid for you all night."

She shook as she stuttered, "CR, I must go to the CR."

He released his grip and she slid off the bed.

"Get me a beer," he bellowed, as she stood up.

She grabbed the towel and got him a beer from the mini bar, placing it on the bedside cabinet to avoid his outstretched arm.

"Don't be long," he grunted, as he ripped the ring off the can.

She entered the bathroom and had only one thought—escape—but how? She turned on the shower without stepping in, paying no attention to the blood on her legs. Standing there, shaking and desperate, she looked around—no bra, no panties, no shoes, and her dress was still draped over the chair beside the bed. She looked at herself in the mirror. Her face in the mirror was red and there was a small cut on her lip where his ring had caught her in a blow. She had to get out while he was still tired from his efforts.

Run away was the only thing she could think of.

She took two deep breaths and squeezed open the door without turning off the shower. She looked across the room. He was still lying in bed with the beer can at his lips. She flung the door open, took two large strides toward the bed, hurled the towel at him and grabbed the dress. She made for the door and turned the lock as he screamed at her to get back. She opened the door and dashed into the corridor just as she heard the beer can crash against the woodwork of the door. She ran to the lifts, glancing back for a fraction of a second to see him in hot pursuit, struggling to hold onto the towel wrapped around his waist. Even in this panic, she had the sense not to take the lift, but forced the fire exit door open and leapt down the stairs four at a time, all the while listening for the noise of the fire door behind her. It did not come. She stopped, feeling her heart jumping inside her. Only then, with the thought of her nakedness, did she slip the dress over her head and descend the remaining stairs. But if he had not followed her into the stairwell, he might have taken the lift and be waiting for her on the ground floor. She rushed to think of a plan.

She had been in this hotel before but had only used the main door. There had to be another way out, there had to be. As she got to the ground floor she saw the sign for the lobby, but the stairs continued down so she followed them. A further flight down and she saw the sign "Staff Exit". Her heart leapt with relief. She opened the door to a corridor. She followed it and passed two changing rooms marked "male" and "female", then turned a corner. Right at the end was a security desk. She thought about running straight to the guard and telling him what had happened. But what if her attacker was a well-known customer? He could say she tried to steal from him or something like that. No, she must keep running.

In the noiseless corridor her lack of shoes helped her move silently. Just as the guard looked up from the newspaper, she bolted for the door and ran outside, feeling the humid air rush into her lungs. She ran on, paying no attention to the guard calling to her from the door.

She slowed down, feeling safe. Then the reality of her situation set in—no money, no purse and hardly any clothes on. Her first thought was the police but the mamas had always told us never to involve the police in anything. She slipped down into a quiet backstreet and continued until she came to a familiar landmark.

There was no avoiding the bright lights of Lockhart Road, so she huddled her arms across her chest and tried to keep in the shadows as she made her way back toward the bar.

Our first knowledge of trouble was when we saw Sheena being helped into the bar by the doorman. We stared at her as she made her way barefoot and in obvious shock toward the changing room. I jumped from the stage, ignoring the mamas' calls for me to remain. In the quiet and safety of the changing room, she told us briefly what had happened. A mama called to one of the men who monitored the security of the bars and he listened as she spoke in Chinese. She told Sheena to wash at a sink and remain there. I sat cradling her head against me and stroking her hair. I let her cry and cried with her. How could anyone do this sort of thing to such a pretty girl?

It was not until the next morning that we heard the mama had gone to the hotel with one of the men to retrieve Sheena's things. The mama told us that they had reported him to the police and that action would be taken. I don't think any action was ever taken. To this day I believe that the mama worked the situation to her advantage to get more money out of the man, using the threat of police as her weapon.

Sheena checked her handbag and purse. The watch she had proudly bought was gone, her photographs of her family torn up, her makeup smashed and he had urinated inside the bag. She threw it away and burst into tears. But the thing that upset Sheena the most about the whole episode must have been the way Mimi reacted. It was as if she blamed Sheena for what had happened. Sheena's face was full of bruises and she couldn't really work in the bar but Mimi showed no sympathy. "If you can't work, you won't get paid." This upset Sheena. Nobody except us girls seemed to care. Sheena was made to remain at home in the apartment by herself while we went to work. The ever watchful Rose kept popping in and out, making sure she didn't leave. After three days Sheena was so bored she pleaded with Mimi to let her come back to the bar. Her face was still bruised but Mimi said okay, provided she put on extra makeup to hide some of the marks.

In a day the story was around the other bars and reaction set in. We had all seen Sheena's customer. He looked normal. He was well dressed, reasonably good looking and never moaned about the money. He had talked nicely to Sheena, had not shown any sign of what was lurking inside. So how can you ever be sure? When that hotel door closes behind you, you are alone.

All of the girls were worried and took no notice of the mamas trying to play down the incident. They had seen what it had done to Sheena and they did not want the same experience. Over the next few weeks or so, the girls were going out less and less on bar fines. The managers and mamasans knew that they had to do something to relieve the fears of the girls and bring back their profits.

They decided that if the girl was not sure about a customer but still wanted to go out, then one of the mamas would go with them as a kind of escort. She would check out the man and make sure he was known in the hotel. If all was okay she would leave them to it. If it was a short-time affair she would either wait there or return a few hours later. In any event, they promised to get a copy of his credit card and phone the hotel to confirm he was staying there. The reality was that most of the girls needed money. The managers needed it too. And even with these additional security measures, deep down we all knew that if it was going to happen again, it would.

Slowly things got back to normal. Sheena did not go out for several weeks, and who could blame her? But ultimately the need for money would win, forcing her to break through the fear and go out again.

This was one of the most frightening incidents that happened at our bar during my stay in Hong Kong, but it was not the only terrifying event. One of the girls working in Carnival Club was subjected to a more horrifying experience. An Indian man had bought her several drinks and then paid her bar fine. Again all the girls said he looked normal, covered in gold jewellery and obviously rich. When she got to the hotel room with him she found two other men already undressed and in bed. She tried to get away but was punched in the stomach then stripped of her clothes. She was forced onto the bed and one of them stuffed her panties into her mouth to muffle her screams. They took turns to play with her body, biting her nipples and forcing their hands inside her vagina. One of them even stubbed out his cigarette on her breast. They showed her no mercy. For the next four hours, two of them would hold her down on the bed, forcing her legs apart while the third raped her.

When one was finished another took his place. They went on until they could hurt her no more.

She left the hotel room battered, bruised, bloody and scared out of her mind. As usual, the mamas said they would do something, but in reality they did no more than talk about it. When her six months were up she refused to renew her contract, even though desperate for money. She returned home to a life filled with uncertainty, still poor and with such bad memories of Hong Kong. We never heard from her again.

12. Clearer Days

Hong Kong shares the same latitude as Hawaii and Calcutta, but instead of a tropical climate it shows evidence of four seasons. January and February can be downright chilly. March and April signal spring, bringing warmer weather but trading off these benefits with occasional rain. June ushers in the summer monsoon, what the Chinese call "plum rains". Summer is a mixture of sun and thunderstorms. In July and August, temperatures average 33° Celsius and humidity can hold at 90 percent. It is said that one has not lived in Hong Kong until one has survived summer and been "baptised by fire". Finally, by mid-September the weather breaks and with the change come cooler, clearer days with a near absence of rain. October and November are the golden months when the view from Hong Kong Island's Peak is as spectacular as tourism photographs.

WITH SEPTEMBER UPON US and our six months almost up, we were asked to extend our contract for the final six months. I knew I had to. I had been out on two more bar fines since the Japanese man, and though I had been able to send money home and my brother was a lot better, it still was not enough to make our lives at home more comfortable. I signed along with all the rest and resigned myself to the next six months.

The week after, one of the managers called a meeting. He told us that some people were going to visit the bar in the next day or so. They were looking for some girls to go to Europe and Canada to work in the bars there. "The money there is a lot more than you can earn here," he said. "They only want four girls for Canada and three for Europe." I did not know whether to feel excited but I could see Sheena's eyes light up while he was talking. Then, for I think the first time, we sampled a taste of honesty. Or perhaps he knew none of us had much dignity left to lose.

"You will work as hostesses and you will have to dance striptease."

Hearing "striptease", I put the thought of another country right out of my head. Dancing naked was certainly not for me. He told us he had no influence over the selectors but he would arrange the contract. As it turned out, he also got a commission from the "buyers" of these girls.

A few days later, two men and a very well dressed woman turned up. We immediately knew who they were from the royal treatment the manager gave them. They sat there for a good hour until they had watched all the girls dance. Every now and again they would ask for the name of a girl and write it down. I found their staring at us a little disturbing, even after all this time. It was like being on a fashion parade except that they were not interested in the clothes, just what was inside them. Apparently, they spent two nights doing this in all of the bars.

Sheena and I had not been selected but Baby and Mika were. Sheena was disappointed but we were both pleased for Baby and Mika. My cousin Roseanna had also been selected. The others on the list I did not know that well. The girls had two days to make up their minds. If they agreed to go, the contracts would be signed and the paperwork started.

Mika and Baby decided not to go. When I asked, Baby said it was too far and Canada was too cold. I know I could not have survived there by myself and I think Baby recognised this too. Coming to Hong Kong was bad enough, but to travel to the other side of the world would require greater courage and spirit. Roseanna said she would go and told me it was for "the money". She said that it couldn't be any worse than what we already did. I wished her luck and promised a going-away party. It does not do much good to try to understand how everybody else thinks. I accepted her decision and understood it was for money.

In the month or so that it took to process their papers, the girls remained in their respective bars. The selectors left Hong Kong and we returned to normal.

We had all noticed a change in Sheena since her bad experience. She was not her normal bubbly self with the customers, being rather cautious. While drinking, she was studying each one, looking for a sign to tell what this guy was really like. Of course there was no way of telling. Outward appearances, we had learnt, show little of what is inside.

A few nights later Sheena was talking to a customer and I guess the subject of him taking her out came up. After her next dance he was still sitting there waiting for her. She excused herself, saying she needed to go to the bathroom. As she passed me, she asked me to follow her.

"If I can get him to take us both out, will you come?"

"What?" I gasped.

I had seen Sheena naked as we showered together, but the thought of sex with another girl there, however close I was to her, shocked me.

"Don't worry," she said. "He seems very nice and I promise I won't let him touch you if you don't want to."

"No, Sheena, I couldn't do that."

"Oh come on," she pleaded. "I am still frightened to go out by myself."

This would be the first time out for her with a customer she did not know after that dreadful event.

"Come on," she said again, when I remained silent. "I need the money."

I thought about the times she had stood up for me and how much she had given to our group.

"All right," I said, "but I don't want him inside me."

She kissed me and thanked me, saying she would love me forever. We returned to the bar.

She told me that if he agreed to pay both our bar fines, she would do all the "work" and would not let him touch me. All I would have to do is join in the fun.

I looked at him. He looked back and smiled. He seemed nice and had already bought Sheena four drinks. They called me over and he bought me a drink. Money was obviously not a problem. We talked for a while. I was watching Sheena and thinking how desperate she was for money, yet was still worried about what had happened before. I spoke to her in Pampangan and told her again that as long as she promised to do everything, I would go. He was obviously interested in going out with Sheena but it was now a question of whether he would go for two bar fines.

I held his hand while Sheena danced. She was really working him. The tattoo, the slow body movements, the glancing eyes—she was putting everything into it. I stroked his arm, watching the two of them smile at each other. She pointed at him, then at me, and then pointed to herself. He looked confused. She held up two fingers, then four, then one. He still looked confused. She smiled, stepped down from the stage and whispered in his ear. "Two Four One," and added, "two girls for one man." She hopped back onto the stage. He laughed, realising what she meant. As she moved into her last dance song, she repeatedly did the two-four-one sign. She blew him a kiss as she stepped back down and went to get her shirt.

She sat down, kissed him gently and put on those big pleading eyes that she had used so many times before. She even sulked a little to make him feel sorry for her. In no time, he had negotiated a good discount for us two girls from the mama, who of course made sure he bought us another drink before we were allowed to get changed.

We sat on either side of him for the short ride to the Hilton. We smiled at the doorman. Thoughts of my first time in this hotel flooded back, but this time I felt different. I had Sheena next to me.

He had not said much since we left the bar but as the lift doors opened he smiled at us and said, "I must be crazy to be doing this." He squeezed our hands and we followed him to his room.

He told us that if we wanted to take a shower to help ourselves. He sat down on the bed and turned on the TV to a movie channel. We locked the door behind us and I faced Sheena. "Sheena, please don't get me into trouble with this man. I really don't want to do it," I pleaded, holding her hands.

"Don't worry," she said. "You leave your bra and panties on and touch him. I will do everything else."

She promised me three times. We showered together. I slipped my bra and panties back on and she wrapped the huge white towel around her slim body.

He was half lying against the pillows in just his trousers. Sheena joined him on one side. Somewhat nervously I took the other.

"What do you want us to do?" she asked.

"Just play with me," he said.

Sheena was already unbuckling his belt. He slid down the bed from his half-seated position. He put his arm around my waist and the other on the back of Sheena, who was busy slipping off his briefs.

I looked at his erect penis and Sheena took it in her hand. She told me to kiss him, pointing to his nipples. So I kissed him. I did not watch Sheena but I could hear him moaning with pleasure. Sheena told me to get some body lotion from the shower room and I slipped off the bed, returning with the small bottle.

"Put some on your hand," she said in Tagalog, "and do what I do."

Smiling, she slid her hand up and down and around his testicles. He closed his eyes and smiled. Sheena rubbed his chest with her other hand, gently pinching his nipples. I followed suit, dragging my hands gently down the middle of his chest and down the sides of his body until he arched his back. I kissed his nipples, gliding my nails back up the sides of his legs. Sheena kissed the other nipple and continued to stroke him slowly. He gasped, then jerked back a little. "Get some tissue," said Sheena softly, slowing down the motion of her hands.

He still had his eyes closed and a warm smile on his face. Sheena gently wiped him and gave him a kiss. We both sat there for a few moments touching his body. I was wondering what would come next. Did he expect more—if so, what?

"Do you want us to stay the night?" asked Sheena.

He opened his eyes. "No, that's okay."

"Do you want to make love to me?" Sheena said, offering her body toward him. He looked at her nakedness and smiled.

"You're both very beautiful, but no, I'm happy. I have a very busy schedule tomorrow."

So we just sat, me in my underwear and Sheena naked. He caressed both of our bodies for a while, then said, "Pass me that briefcase over there."

I got the bag for him. He fished around and brought out a wallet.

We had not asked for money but he placed a one hundred American dollar bill in each of our hands. He sat up, kissed us both very gently on the lips and said, "You are both very nice, too nice to be working in a bar." He caressed our bodies for the last time, looking at us as if trying to store away a picture. "Buy yourselves something nice." He lay back down and said he was tired. "You can go if you want to—and thank you."

Sheena kissed him in thanks and I did the same. We dressed, talking quietly so as not to disturb him. When we returned from the shower, he was fast asleep. In his hand was his wallet and we could both see a large number of dollar bills inside. We would never touch his money, however, or do anything bad to someone like him. Sheena pulled the covers up over him and kissed his forehead and we left.

In the lift I said, "I would have let him if he had wanted to."

"I know," she said. "He was one of the nice ones."

* * *

I could see Sheena was happy and she had overcome her fear about going out and would soon be able to take on the world again. It was the easiest money I had ever made and one of the few pleasant experiences I would have involving sex and the bar.

"What shall we do now?" she said, as we climbed into the taxi. "No point going straight back to the bar. Mama thinks we are out for the night."

"I don't know."

She asked me how much Hong Kong money I had on me. "About five hundred," I answered.

She counted the notes in her purse.

"Let's go to Lan Kwai Fong," she said, and told the driver to change his direction. We had heard that Lan Kwai Fong was the "in place" and that there were many bars and restaurants.

"We both deserve a night out," she said. The sparkle in her eyes confirmed that her old spirit had returned.

"It's a shame Baby's not here," I replied.

The driver pulled over on a very steep slope and we got out. It was two o'clock, still early, and there were many people about.

Everything looked so modern and rich. It was an amazing mix of uniquely fashioned bars and restaurants and wealthy looking party goers.

Foreigners and Chinese stood in the street holding drinks, chatting away in different languages. It looked busy yet relaxed. We followed the red cobblestone street up the hill to what looked to be the very heart of the bar area. Most of the restaurants had names we couldn't pronounce but their decorations and front signs helped us guess their specialties. We followed the road further up the hill and around the bend, then turned downhill toward the bars again. We were ready for a drink. We decided on Scotties Bar—for one thing, we could pronounce it and it looked quieter than the other bars.

There were maybe ten people inside. A few people stopped talking and glanced at us as we entered. No sooner had Sheena sat at a table did a Filipino waitress address us in Tagalog. Sheena, crazy as ever, ordered a beer. I asked for a fruit punch. Most of the patrons were men but there were two couples sitting near the window, holding hands across the table, locked in deep conversation.

Sheena whispered, "Don't tell anyone what we do, if they ask."

The drinks came and Sheena asked for peanuts. The girl nodded and went to get them.

"Cheers, my one and only best friend," said Sheena, raising her glass.

"Cheers," I returned.

I was happy for Sheena. Her smile, her eyes, her whole posture said *I'm back*.

We listened to music for a while, then two men who were sitting at the bar came over and sat down at our table.

"What are your names?" asked one.

Sheena told them and asked, "So what're yours?"

"Pete" and "Mike," were the replies.

They smiled. "Can we get you a drink?"

I could not believe this was happening.

"Another Budweiser," Sheena said, sipping the last from her glass. "And you?"

"Just fruit punch, thanks."

Mike, who had sat himself next to me, said, "Why don't you have something stronger?"

"Yes, go on," urged Sheena.

After two minutes of pressure I agreed to have a beer as well.

I had never drunk beer before. Well, maybe once. As a child I drank some beer from a bottle that my father had not finished and it tasted terrible. This beer was cool and sweet.

We all said *cheers!* and fell into conversation. A conversation so natural compared with what we were accustomed to in the bar. Sheena told them we were both with Philippine Airlines. "Here on training." We were a little stuck when they asked where we were staying, but once again Sheena improvised. "The airline has a small apartment in Mid Levels, off Robinson Road." She made it sound so realistic that I had trouble keeping a straight face. Don't ask me if it was the beer or the nice man now asleep in the Hilton, but I hadn't had so much fun in a long time.

Mike asked me if I wanted to dance. They were playing *Moonlight Shadow*, a slow ballad.

"Yes, come on."

Pete pulled Sheena to her feet. He moved a table out of the way and created our own little dance floor. Mike put his arm around me and danced with his cheek against mine. The music and the feeling of being treated like a real woman was pure pleasure. Like a nice dream being replayed, I can hear the words of the song echo again.

Carried away by a moonlight shadow,
Lost in a river last Saturday night,
Far away on the other side

Star was light in silvery night,
And she couldn't find how to push through...

I did not even hear the music stop until he squeezed me.

"How long are you here for?" he whispered.

Sheena may have told Pete something. So I said, "We are still waiting to hear."

"Maybe we can get together another night." He squeezed me again and walked me back to the table.

"Maybe," I said.

They asked for our office number. Sheena said we could not give it out because they did not like personal calls. "But if you give us your numbers, we will call you."

"One more drink," they offered. I instinctively refused but under pressure accepted. I could see Sheena was enjoying all of this. To tell the truth, so was I.

This was the first time in my life that anybody other than my family and close friends had shown me tenderness. He may not have meant it but at the time it felt so nice to be treated that way. Mike was kind, handsome in a way and talked to me as a person, not as a bar object. I remembered what my sister had said about giving up her virginity— about feeling grown up and being treated as a normal person.

Four o'clock arrived and we were the only ones in the bar. The owner said he would be closing soon and did we want any more to drink? The boys looked at us. We said we had better be getting back. Ten minutes later we were walking down the steep road toward Central, where they told us we had a better chance of getting a taxi. Sheena was in front with Pete's arm around her shoulders. Mike was holding me around the waist. His touch was different from the others I had experienced. It did not have any sexual undertones.

We stood on the corner, Mike trying to wave down a taxi. I saw Sheena and Pete kissing. Mike pulled me toward him and kissed me on the lips. He was so gentle and soft, not forcing himself on me. This was my first real kiss and the memory of it would remain with me for some time. He kissed me three more times while we waited. It felt so good. I would have been happy to wait for a taxi all night.

"Call me," Mike said. I watched him as the taxi pulled away.

"What a night," I said, sinking back into the seat of our taxi.

"Are you a little drunk?" Sheena asked.

"I don't think so." *But was I light-headed because of the beer or the kisses from Mike?* I looked over my shoulder through the back window and returned one last wave. Sheena just giggled. *Hong Kong isn't so bad after all,* I thought.

We talked about whether to call them and how to find time to meet them. The resurrected Sheena was all for taking a chance. I was less keen, though the thought of meeting Mike again sent a small shiver of excitement through me. But time would always be our problem because we had none, and now that I had got Mimi off my back, I wanted to keep it that way.

That was the only time I ever went out with another girl and a customer. A few of the other girls did, from time to time, normally with a rich businessman. But for some reason it never worked out that a customer liked Sheena and me at the same time.

We never saw our American friend again, but with the money he had given us, both Sheena and I treated ourselves. I bought some perfume and, at last, a camera, and she bought an imitation Rolex watch. We told Baby about our night out together, especially the part about Mike and Pete in Scotties Bar. And we all speculated on whether it would ever be possible to find a customer who would pay all three of our bar fines!

13. Bird Garden

Hong Kong's Yuen Po Street in Prince Edward is known as "bird garden". Old Chinese men gather and pass the time of day by showing off their prize finches. The locals have long favoured birds as pets, seeing them as harbingers of luck. Cages are often ornate and constructed from teak or rosewood but none is too large for its owner to carry. It is easy to spot a bird that has been with its owner for a while. A younger, newly bought bird will dart around in its cage, unable to find a sense of rhythm. A seasoned bird, in the company of its owner, will move with a sense of harmony and confidence. Such a bird flits from lower ledge to upper ledge and from front to back with elegance and effortlessness. This makes the one-by-two-foot cage seem bigger and gives the impression that the bird is not confined by its cage.

FOR THE NEXT FEW WEEKS Sheena pushed me to phone the boys and though I really wanted to, I kept resisting. I had dreamt of how Mike had held and kissed me. I have to confess I even dreamt what it might feel like to make love with him, someone who wanted me because it was me and not just a nice ornament he had seen on the stage. Sheena even said that she would pretend to be ill and ask for me to accompany her to the doctors.

"It's easy," she said. "I will tell Mimi that I think I have caught something." But again I refused her. Though we never fell out over the incident, I know she thought I was silly. Maybe I was, but I thought about what I had become. Going out with someone I liked, making love and then feeling involved and loved; these were feelings that I could only imagine. For if I did get involved with someone like Mike, I knew I would never be able to get back up on that stage and dance again, let alone go out on the occasional bar fine. For me, love and being involved had to wait. There was no way to mix it with my bar work.

* * *

With the realisation of what I had now become—a bar girl—and with the true feelings of affection I had absorbed from my brief meeting with Mike, I still struggled in my mind to fully accept my situation. As in most things, however, comfort and, to some extent, understanding can be found in simple things. For me, it came from some of the music played in the bar. There was one song that had become something of a theme song for us girls. Every girl liked it for different reasons. Some of the girls used it as a chance to dance with slow sensual movements in front of their customers. I liked it for its pure words. It was not exactly a love song but it did have a slow, deep beat.

Tonight,
There'll be no darkness tonight,
Hold tight,
Let your love light shine bright,

Listen to my heart,
And lay your body next to mine,
Let me fill your soul with all my dreams,

You're a woman, I'm a man,
This is more than just a game,
I can make you feel so right,
Be my lady of the night...

I enjoyed dancing to this song. It was sensual and I could close my eyes and think of Mike while swaying to the rhythm. I could hear the words speaking to the feelings deep within me.

I had seen so much and suffered much during those first six months and now time had flown by and we were well into our last six months. The prospect of bar work, dancing and even the occasional bar fine was commonplace to me now. I was always very careful with whom to go out. Unlike Mika, who had since had another abortion, I would never be a "first night stand" girl. If the man truly wanted me, then he had to come back to the bar more than once. If it was just a quick "bonk", as described to me by one Englishman, I was not interested. There was always Mika and one or two of the others who would willingly oblige.

Looking back, I think I was lucky. I had managed to build up a relationship, if you can call it that, with two regular men. They visited the bar now and again and we got to know each other, so going out on the odd bar fine with them was not that much of an ordeal. Both of them were married, and there was no luxury hotel or overnight stay. A few hours in one of the local hotels, and normally always before one or two o'clock. I still worked the customers to get drinks but would save myself until one of my friends came in. On two occasions they both came in on the same night! I did my best to explain later to the one that I was not sitting with at the time, but I think they were both a bit jealous. It made me feel quite nice seeing two men both wanting me, if only for brief companionship. Both of them were extremely kind to me. I think they understood how much I detested what I was doing but we never discussed it. They both bought me a small present for my birthday. One was a small gold necklace with a heart on it, the other a three-coloured gold bracelet. I never asked them about their families and they never questioned me about my work or mine. We just shared brief moments together, a simple uncomplicated relationship that provided me with the extra money and provided them with a little pleasure.

The various navies—British, Australian and US mostly—came and went, causing more trouble and hard work for us girls. Sheena fell in love with one of them who, like most, turned out to be married. He strung her along saying he would leave his wife and how he had never met anyone like her. She even took a chance and met him outside the bar on a few occasions, knowing that the mamas were so busy with the other sailors and there was less chance of her getting caught. They would go to a hotel, make love and talk about their future. She was completely wrapped up with his promises. When they all left, he promised to write. He did send one letter a few months later, saying he was sorry but he was going to stay with his wife. As usual, she took it well, throwing it off as another experience. She told me later that night, when we were alone, that she really thought he was going to be the one.

Shortly after his letter, I could see she was still upset, and when Mama told us we could leave early that night, I decided to take her out, and to hell with Rose and Mimi. When we were in the taxi and before Sheena could say "Quarry Bay", I said "Lan Kwai Fong". Sheena and Baby turned and looked at me, so I smiled and said it again. Sheena chuckled. She was always ready to take a chance. "We deserve it," I said, "and if we get caught, so what?"

We took Baby around Lan Kwai Fong and the bars, having a few beers along the way. We popped into Scotties; Sheena had insisted, but the boys were not there. A few other guys tried to chat us up. We let them buy us a drink and even went through the Philippine Airlines story with them. Baby laughed at my exaggeration and joined in. She told them that if one of us got promoted we were going to celebrate by having a house party. Here we were in control. We were able to go into a bar, meet who we wanted and leave when we wanted. By the end of the night Baby was drunk and was sick in the street, but despite that she really enjoyed it.

At moments like this, when we were free and could enjoy ourselves, I realised that some of the good stories I had heard before I left for Hong Kong really were true. I wondered why the bar managers did not let us girls go out by ourselves. It would have made life in the bar so much more bearable. Perhaps the temptation of "real" men outside the bar would have been too much for many of the girls. Yes, they had to control our lives including where we could or could not spend our time, or else many of the girls would see the real side of Hong Kong social life, and would want it.

We were to do the Lan Kwai Fong trip another four or five times before we left Hong Kong, and we only got caught once. We had told Mimi that the taxi had broken down and we had to walk. She did not believe us and we did get fined, but it was well worth it.

My cousin Roseanna left us to go to Canada and we did throw a party for her and the other girls who were leaving. All the girls chipped in with a little money and we bought a cake, beer and crisps, and even paid Rose (our cook and "guardian") to make us a special meal. Mimi allowed me to take Roseanna to the airport and we parted in tears, promising each other to write as often as we could.

Several new girls arrived at different stages and others left. The mamas turned their attention to the new girls. This new "flesh" was prized, at least for the first few months. We would hear the mamas talking about and pointing out the new girls to the customers. "New girls ... fresh ... from the province." It made me cringe, for not so long ago it was me they were describing. Moreover, it was noticeable that the customers did show more interest and attention to the new girls.

I continued to send money home and post letters with pictures of us in Hong Kong so that my parents could show them to their friends. I was still careful with money but was able to buy some nice things for myself. Other than the camera, I now had a watch, a cassette player and what I thought were some reasonable clothes. I never could afford to shop in Pacific Place but I found that, by waiting for the sales, I could pick up some good bargains at many of the local shops and occasionally in World Wide Plaza when we went there to transfer money home. Perhaps the most important function of World Wide Plaza was to assist in the remittance of funds to the Philippines. Every week, hundreds of thousands of dollars flowed from Hong Kong back to the Philippines.

* * *

I had been to World Wide Plaza almost every month but had never really stopped to explore the complex. I would go at midweek when the place was less busy to make a money transfer and buy a Philippine newspaper, then head straight back to our apartment. This particular day was Sunday—the busiest day of the week. I arrived at the Equitable Bank located inside the Plaza and glanced at the exchange rate. The peso rate for today looked favourable. I wondered how long banks such as Equitable, BPI, PNB and Metro had been here in Hong Kong, crowded into World Wide Plaza. I took my place in line and could already feel the pace slowing down. Watching the staff behind the bank counter, it appeared to me as if my clerk was performing his duties in slow motion. I had in some respects become used to the quick pace of Hong Kong life, be it the aggressive way the mamasans operated in the bar or the fast service in the Chinese restaurants located around where we lived.

My transaction done, I went for a stroll. The many small stores in World Wide Plaza catered almost exclusively to the overseas Hong Kong Filipino community. While the most obvious businesses were banks, travel and airline booking services, and long distance telephone phone card services, there were also diverse other shops selling clothing, jewellery, music, stationery, books and alteration services. Adjacent to Franki Exchange was the Philippines Products Store stocking little cans of familiar products—canned squid and potato paste—all lined up in cute rows.

World Wide Plaza consisted of three floors and the shops were small even by Hong Kong standards. I guessed them to be around 6 to 8 feet wide. Shop No. 175, Unique Products Store, sold cheap cosmetics. The only unique thing appeared to be the "Breast Enlargement Cream" advertised in its front window. Some products were offered with a plastic watch as a "Free gift!" I wondered how good a watch could be if it was given away free.

Pilipino was the language all around me in this Pinoy enclave. Music tapes played English songs, Tagalog songs and familiar English songs dubbed over in Tagalog. There were English and Tagalog videos for purchase or rent, as well as videos for Tagalog and English karaoke, and even Christian karaoke.

I was now on the third floor, revelling in names of more diverse shops: the Automatic Embroidery Shop employed an automatic embroidery machine, which printed on shirts or towels pre-selected phrases like "Love You Forever" or "From Tiny to Teddie Always". I browsed the front windows of the Perfect Shoe Service, Sari-Sari Store, Sisters Bra Shop, and Perfect Fashion Alteration Shop. Benjamin's Bookshop contained more religious cards than actual books and Victory Jewellery Co. did not have much of a jewellery collection but instead sold and rented romance books. What must once have been a large jewellery collection had been reduced to a single jewellery counter near the cash register. I only had time to glance at the book covers, predictable romance titles like *Two Hearts to Lose* featuring a couple embracing on the front cover and *Macho Rider* with a man on horseback and a woman staring out from a barn. I wondered how long it had been since I read anything because bar life had been so all-consuming.

I discovered a small shop tucked away in the corner. Shop No. 358 was Little Divisoria. Although tiny, it had a counter to accommodate those who didn't mind eating their food standing up. Ordering dried fish and rice with vegetable, I almost thought I was back in the Philippines.

I left World Wide Plaza pleased that I had taken the time to explore it. It had so amused me that I continued to walk through Central for a closer look at the Sunday activities. On the Lord's day the area around Central was the designated meeting place for Filipino overseas workers. Chater Road was closed to traffic, and behind the temporary yellow and black "road closed" barrier Filipinos could safely take over their Sunday sanctuary. I found myself living a "Filipino Sunday". It seemed as if all of the approximately 200,000 Filipinos who were working in Hong Kong were now right here in Central. Almost everyone was female and almost everyone was a domestic helper. I stopped and stood in front of Prince's Building, observing all the women sitting in groups, chatting and eating. It reminded me of Fiesta time in the Philippines.

I noticed a girl standing next to me reading a romance book like the one I had seen in the Plaza. We started talking and I realised she shared a similar dialect, being from a nearby province in the Philippines. She explained to me that despite the mob-like gathering there were actual places in Central where girls from different regions of the Philippines gathered on Sundays to get news and rehash gossip. The Panpanguenos, those from the central plains of Luzon, preferred to meet at the north end of Chater Garden, while the southern end of the Garden was home to those from Zambales. The paving underneath the Hong Kong Bank, famous for its glass underside, is where you could find Cebuanos from Cebu, and the Ifugaos originating from Baguio stretched along the pathway that led from Prince's Building down to the MTR station. The Cagayanos from the northwest of the Philippines laid temporary claim to the area around Star Ferry, while a short distance away, around City Hall, you found the Illongos, mostly from the Ilo Ilo area. And so it went, different people from different provinces spreading themselves around Central. It seemed so strange that these ethnic groups had "printed" their own gigantic map of the Philippines and blanketed it over the Central district of Hong Kong. On Sunday you might well have thought yourself back in the Philippines. But by Monday the road barriers were removed, the streets cleaned and Central was handed back to the businessmen and shopkeepers.

After we spoke for a while, I proceeded to move into Chater Garden itself and observe a world that until now had remained hidden from me, just as my world was hidden from others. Some girls were having their own church service right on the lawn, with one girl standing and reading to them. Others were singing hymns in groups. Some were locked in meditation with their eyes closed. Others were lying down sleeping. Some girls were dressed up but most of the girls and the few Filipino guys were in jeans and tee shirts. I caught fragments of conversations, with one person saying "See you in one hour" and another responding "at the lion statue".

There were girls cutting hair, braiding hair, perming hair, taking photographs, exchanging pamphlets, reading books, selling shirts, selling bags, checking blood pressure, telling jokes—just about everything I could think of. And of course many were eating. There were strange smells in the air. Filipino snacks of fried pigskin, purple yam candy, fried glutinous rice, demerara sugar balls on skewers and mixed fruit and ice drinks that I easily recognised as *halo-halo*. With so much finger food around, the ingenious system of finger bags was in full operation. Messy food was sold with a transparent plastic glove. The customer slipped on the glove and held the food with that hand. Upon finishing, any bones left over were simply caught in the glove as it was rolled back off the hand in reverse fashion. Although this made me feel homesick, the colourful world I was only beginning to uncover would soon be a memory.

* * *

With our contract time running out, I sensed Sheena's and even Baby's increased efforts to get more bar fines. I guess they thought it was the last opportunity to take back some extra money. I stuck to my two regulars and was happy with that arrangement. We had already been told that next month we would have to go back but the date was not fixed.

Like the other mamas, Mimi had turned her attention toward the new girls but she was still there pushing us. I knew she could not hurt me any more, but as usual she would take whatever opportunity came along to make money, and whenever possible at my expense. I wondered whether she had forgiven me for being difficult in the early days.

She knew how I detested going to the booths, yet even though I had almost finished my time in Hong Kong, on at least two occasions in the last month she forced me to spend time there with a customer. It was just her way of showing me that she could still manipulate me. Then one night she really got me. The bar was particularly busy and Sheena, Baby and Mika had already gone out. I was rushing around doing my best and hardly noticed two very drunk Japanese men sitting at the bar. They were sitting with a new girl and the pot was full of drink tickets. Such was the shortage of girls that night that there were only two on the stage dancing; the others were fully occupied with customers.

Mimi shouted at me across the bar to bring drinks. It annoyed me that she should still treat me like this, especially with the new girls in the bar able to hear her shouting. I went over with two bottles of beer.

"Whiskey, you stupid girl," she shouted, pushing me away.

My rage returned. I wanted to drop the bottles on the floor and walk out. But I turned, feeling the embarrassed flush on my face, got the drinks and placed them in front of the men and left. Mimi laughed and I knew she was saying something about me. Then I heard my name being called again. Like a slave I returned, not smiling, just standing there waiting.

"Get changed," she said. "This man has paid your bar fine." I was shocked. I had not even thought of him as a customer, he had not bought me a drink and I had not even said hello to him.

"Get changed," she said, even louder. "Tonight—"

What could I do? I walked back to the changing room, all my hatred returning. I had thought she had accepted my way of bar life—my two regulars and the occasional bar fine with someone that I selected. But even in this last month of my tour she appeared determined to demonstrate her dominance over me. For all I know she might have done it on purpose to show the new girls that she was in charge.

I glared at her as I helped the man from his stool. He could hardly stand up. The other girl took the arm of his companion and we left the bar. Mimi smiled and wiped the bar, no doubt savouring yet another victory.

We arrived at the hotel and I went through the ritual of showering. I knew he was drunk and when I returned to the room, he was just lying motionless on the bed. I thought about just leaving, then he stirred and sat up.

The next half hour was taken up with him trying his best to have sex with me. There was lots of touching, fondling and kissing. He even managed to get himself inside me once or twice. But he could not sustain his erection. He flopped down on the bed next to me. "We try later," he said. "You sleep now, we try again later." Then I heard him start to snore; he was asleep.

I waited a few more minutes then decided to leave. Thinking that the noise of the shower might wake him up, I decided to shower later and quietly got dressed. I placed the small bottles of complimentary body lotion and shampoo into my bag, picked up my shoes and made for the door. I looked back. He was dead to the world. I knew he would not wake up for hours.

As I left the hotel I had already made up my story in case he later returned to the bar and complained to Mimi. I would simply say that he was too drunk to remember and that we did indeed have sex. In fact, we had had sex three times. That, I knew, would make him feel like a man.

I walked from the Shangri-la Hotel to Central and up to Lan Kwai Fong. The night air was cool and the place almost deserted. It was three o'clock in the morning and I arrived on the chance that Sheena or Baby had finished with their customers and might be there.

I stood at the mouth of Lan Kwai Fong, noting the bars on both sides of the red cobblestone street. I was here alone for the first time and a strange sense of tranquillity came over me. In the daytime, in those rare moments when it is peaceful, there is never the same feeling. But when night is not yet over and morning has not arrived, the night speaks to you and you to it. The cobblestone street made me feel much bigger and the buildings around me seemed smaller. Suddenly I imagined I was a big girl in a small land, standing in a playhouse. It was indeed like a small village consisting of only bars and restaurants, all bunched together where houses would otherwise stand. And a wonderful red checkerboard road circled around the block, ending where it had begun. Yes, it reminded me of a checkerboard! How much fun it would be to place some rocks on the ground and make some moves. I glanced down, angling the toe of my shoe to test the brick's texture. Each block was perfectly connected to the next, not a crack between them. It was as if each red brick was a piece of a giant puzzle. But it was a strange puzzle with no picture on it.

I started walking to snap myself out of this surreal state. I decided to search two or three of the bars we had all visited before, but Sheena and Baby were not to be found. I thought about stopping and having a drink by myself but decided against it.

Then my heart jumped. Was that Mike walking up the hill toward Scotties? My instinct took over and I followed. Memories of that night flooded back—the drinks, dancing, his arms around me as we kissed goodnight. I hesitated just for a moment before entering Scotties. But there he was at the bar. He was talking to a Chinese girl, his hand on her shoulder. Then I saw him give her a kiss.

A jealous rage filled me. I wanted to go over to him but held back. I was still standing there watching when the waitress came over and asked if I wanted a table. Then I saw him turn around. My heart jumped again. It was not Mike but someone who looked so much like him. He stared for a moment and I looked back at him. Then calmness returned. Even if it was Mike, what right did I have to act like this? My one night with him did not give me any rights. I turned and left, feeling stupid.

As I stepped back into the night I felt a flush in my cheeks. Thinking about Mike had brought back nice feelings. Thinking he was with another girl … well that brought feelings of jealousy. I hurried back down the hill and found a taxi. On my way back toward Quarry Bay, I laughed quietly. Was this love I was feeling?

I told Sheena and Baby about the incident later the next day. They laughed about the drunken Japanese guy and told me not to pay any more attention to Mimi.

"She is only doing it because she knows we will soon be gone," Baby said. I knew she was probably right, especially when she added, "Maybe she's doing it because she feels guilty and frustrated."

I wrote and told my family I would soon be home. As I sealed and posted the letter, something jumped inside me. It must have been knowing that soon it would be over. I had put the bad memories away, even Mimi's last demonstration of power. And other than those times when Mimi turned on me, I have to admit to enjoying myself over the last few months. Amid the excitement of going home I felt sad to be leaving Hong Kong. Then at last we were given our date. Only nine more days to go. We were to leave in two groups a few days apart. Our trio—Sheena, Baby and me—were on the same flight. Don't ask me how, but we had managed to stay together from Angeles City to Hong Kong and now back again. It may have been fate or maybe God had something to do with it, but our friendly triangle was intact. And now we were to share our last adventure together—the flight home.

A rush of excitement built up in us all. All three of us had to buy a new case. No way could we fit our things in the little bag that only a year ago had held everything we owned. I had promised my swimsuits to one of the new girls now in our apartment. I felt sorry for her. She was just starting her stint and was probably more nervous than I ever was. Sheena said she was taking hers home with her. "Never know when I might need them again," she said.

Like me, Baby promised hers to one of the others, saying there was no way she would let Mimi get her hands on them to be resold. When I gave mine to the girl, she hugged and thanked me as if I had given her the world. I said she was welcome to them because I knew I would never put them on again.

Two days to go and Mimi gave us our tickets. I asked her where my "dance card" was, the card that I had worked so hard for. She simply told us these would be returned to the promotion. We later learned that the management kept them so that they could use them if necessary for another girl, by simply changing the names.

That night we persuaded Mimi to let us leave early. We had planned a last secret visit to Lan Kwai Fong. We told her we still had to pack and would be very busy tomorrow. She agreed at last, realising that her control over us was finished and now concerned more about the new girls.

Our last night on the town was a storm. I know we all got drunk because I can't remember going home. I recall at one stage Sheena tried to kiss all the men she could find and started a striptease, much to the delight of the men who whistled and cheered her on. She was down to her bra and about to unzip her jeans when I stopped her. They booed me then clapped as Sheena threw her bra into the crowd. I thought there was going to be a riot. With Baby's help, I managed to get her tee shirt back on and sit her down. The manager of the bar brought us drinks.

"Great!" he said. "These are on the house and you can come back and do that any night. It's great for business."

In the end we all left our mark on Hong Kong: Sheena with her impromptu striptease, Baby by being sick again in the taxi home and me—I bashed an overzealous man over the head with a beer bottle, much to the delight of his friends.

Our last day rushed by. With our hangovers that morning, I am sure Mimi knew we got back late. Whether she ignored it or expected it, she did not fine us. We had all checked the purchases on our shopping lists and were busy trying to cram presents into our bags when she came in.

"I know we have had our differences," she said, "but I just wish you luck in the future and I hope to see you again."

She gave each of us a small Chinese statue with a dragon on it. "It is the symbol for long life," she said. We thanked her. Why would she act like that on the last day? Perhaps it was guilt. Someone told me that the Chinese are very superstitious and that leaving someone with bad feelings could affect you for the rest of your life. Maybe this little gift was her way of parting as friends so we would not come back and haunt her. Whatever the reason, we squeezed her dragon into our already bulging cases.

I met Tina one last time to say goodbye and Sheena and Baby came with me. She took us to a Chinese restaurant near Happy Valley and I insisted on paying the bill. She was sad to see me leave and handed me several letters to take back. We wished each other luck before she walked off back to her job and we three jumped on a tram and headed in the opposite direction.

We entered the bar for the final time. We did not have to dance so we just sat and served drinks. I watched the new girl wearing my costume. Did I once look like that—shy, nervous, full of worry at what was ahead?

Mimi let us go at midnight. We considered a last night on the town but knew our bodies would not take it. I for one was so excited at going home and I knew it would be hard to sleep that night.

I gazed for the last time at the Hong Kong night lights as the taxi took us back. I wanted to remember what had once been so different and exciting but had now become commonplace. We sat and talked for at least an hour, not being used to sleeping so early. None of us knew what we were going to do when we got back. All we knew was that we had survived Hong Kong and all that went with the bar scene. The negative experiences would be balanced with memories of the good times.

Morning came and our transport to the airport arrived just after nine. The whole apartment was still asleep. We said a quiet goodbye, left our door keys on the side table for Mimi, collected our bags and closed the door for the last time.

The whole day was then filled with rushing and queuing up in lines at the airport. With all that had happened this past year I had forgotten how busy airports were. We had all saved some money to spend in the duty-free shop. This time we could try on the perfumes and even buy one. I bought a bottle for my mother. For my father I bought a large bottle of brandy. I had during the last few frantic days already bought presents for my brothers and sisters.

Finished with our last bit of shopping, we indulged ourselves in a drink at the little bar. Sheena insisted it should be beer.

"What, at this time of the morning!" said Baby.

"Yes," said Sheena. "Why not?"

* * *

The flight was on time and we boarded without problems. This time Baby took the window seat while I sat in the middle and Sheena by the aisle. As we took to the air, we all squeezed our heads toward the little window to get our last look at the place that had been our home for a year.

I had planned to watch the short film but instead took a nap, having underestimated the fatigue of the last few days and the excitement of going home. I was still dreaming when the stewardess woke me to put my seat upright and check my seatbelt.

"There is turbulence," she said, as she moved on up the aisle. With the plane rising and falling in small jerks, we all held each other's hands. Milky white clouds flashed past the window, interspaced with streaks of blue sky, and each time we passed though these clouds there was a sudden drop, which made our stomachs rise and our hands clasp even tighter. Then we were below the clouds, still bumping along, twisting slightly to the left, then to the right, lower and lower and finally levelling. There was a thud as the wheels skidded on the runway, followed by another, and another, then the engines roared in reverse, thrusting us forward in our seats. A spontaneous cheer went through the cabin, followed by clapping. The stewardess announced, "Welcome to Manila International Airport." We were home.

* * *

After clearing immigration and collecting our bags we pushed past the crowds to find our service man. The last thing the promotion would do for us was to arrange for us to be met by a driver with a jeepney. We had to pay him of course, but he would drive us all the way back to Angeles, where it had all started over a year ago. From there we were on our own.

As we loaded our things into the jeepney, the manager and promotion ripped us off for what would be the last time. The driver collected all our passports, saying that he had to register us back and that they would be returned in a few weeks. We never saw them again. I later heard that the promotion held on to them, using them sometimes to send other girls out of the country.

It was a slow journey back from Manila. The smells and sights that I had grown up with returned to me as we made our way north. It was good to see the palm trees and the rice fields. No more towering buildings, only the peace and quiet of the countryside. We were all melancholy during the journey, having already swapped our addresses and promised to keep in touch. Who could tell if our paths would cross again. Some of the girls I knew I would never see again. But Sheena, Baby and myself—after all the hard times we had endured, I hoped the memories of our good times would serve me well, memories of sharing and the closeness and honesty we had for each other. When I look back on those times, there is one picture which will always bring me comfort. It is the one with Sheena in the middle, Baby and me at her sides resting our heads on her strong shoulders and clasping her hands—a fitting end to our Hong Kong adventure.

* * *

As we arrived in Angeles City, I don't know who spoke first, but as soon as she did we all burst into tears. We must have looked an odd sight to passers-by, kissing and hugging each other. The group dispersed and Sheena, Baby and I remained. Again we promised to write, then we separated and went our different ways.

I caught the bus for the short ride to my village. So many thoughts ran through my head—the sadness of leaving my friends, the excitement of seeing my family again. You would have thought that the sights and sounds of my province would have brought back the memories of home and my family, who were no doubt waiting anxiously for my arrival. Nevertheless, my thoughts kept drifting back to the bonding experiences of Hong Kong. It was a strange feeling realising that I was returning a stronger person.

I stepped down from the bus and into a waiting tricycle. I blurted instructions to the driver and the trike's engine roared into life and we were thrust forward. Soon we turned down the road where my old school stood. I looked up at the silhouette outlining the long line of classroom windows. I had once stood behind those windows and looked out over the distant fields dreaming of a future.

There was an unbelievable rush of people as the tricycle turned into the driveway. Tears were in everybody's eyes. All my family were hugging me at the same time. I could hardly keep my balance. My brother took my case and bag and somehow we all made it inside. As I sat down on the sofa I could see two laminated pictures on the wall. One was of Sheena, Baby and me standing outside Quarry Bay MTR station and the other was of me sitting on my bunk bed in the apartment—the first pictures we had taken with Sheena's camera. Looking at those pictures, Hong Kong now seemed more than a hundred thousand miles away.

With so much to catch up on, everyone was talking at once. My father, also with tears in his eyes, ordered the children out of the room, saying that there was plenty of time later for them to talk to me. My mother sat with her hands on my knees. All she kept saying was, "Are you all right?" My sister sat with her arm around me. I was home at last.

Happy yet exhausted, I asked my brother to bring out my case. I thought that handing out the presents would give me time to compose myself. I was wrong. Hearing about the presents, the children were back in the house. For each gift there were tears and thank you's, then more tears.

My mother, being her typical self, had prepared a huge meal and when we sat down to eat she made us all say a prayer of thanks for my safe return. I looked around the table at the faces of my family and then in silence said my own prayer of thanks.

"We have rice and mangoes growing," my father announced after dinner. He had bought a small piece of land with the money I'd sent back. He was proud not just of me but also of what he had been able to do.

I told my mother when we were alone that I wanted to visit the grave of my grandmother. She said she would come with me once everything had been cleaned up. As we walked down the road, she holding my hand, I nodded and said hello to all the people who greeted me but we did not stop until we reached the graveyard. As we turned into the graveyard I could sense the peace of the place. We paid our respects and I quietly thanked my grandmother for all the help she had given me spiritually, and promised to visit as often as I could. As we walked slowly back to the house my mother said how pretty my necklace was. I told her I had bought it at a market in Hong Kong. I could never say where it really came from.

She told me that Eddie was so much better, thanks to me. He had worn a supporting leg brace for a while and would always have a small limp when he walked but at least he was all right. She must have thanked me a hundred times. She cried when she told me how helpless she felt when all of this was going on, how she hated asking me for money. It was, she told me over and over again, the only thing she could think of.

"If it was not for you, who knows what would have happened to him."

I told her that it was all right and not to think of it any more. "At least he is well again and I am so happy I could help," I said.

Her talking to me that way brought back some of the bad feelings I had toward my father and the fact that I had to make sacrifices because he was unable to cope. But even now, thinking of Eddie, I know that what I had to go through had not been for nothing.

My mother never asked me about what really went on in Hong Kong. I guess deep down she knew and understood. When the subject did come up I spared her the horror stories, passing them off as just another experience. I spent most of my time telling her about my friends and how we had all enjoyed Hong Kong, though she was a little shocked when I told her that I had been drinking beer. My sister, on the other hand, wanted to know everything. Later that evening, as we sat together outside, I told her some of it, but again I kept the worst parts to myself, knowing that she would have felt bad. For if not for her pregnancy it might well have been her.

As for my father, he seemed to have become a new man. He had through my help been able to again find his dignity and self-respect. When he showed me the small farm, he walked along with me, his arm around my shoulders. As we stood there looking at the green shoots of rice pushing their way upward to the sky, he said, "I know it was hard for you but if there had been any other way—"

I stopped him and said, "Father, it's all right. I love you and I always will."

He turned his head away not wanting me to see him cry. I know he knew what went on and what I had been expected to do. But I forgave him. As we walked back he said, "I am going to buy two pigs next week."

That night, after my sister and I finished talking, we went back inside the house. My father had been able to build another small room onto one side of the house. This was to become my new bedroom. I don't think he built it out of guilt but rather because I deserved it. No longer was I crammed into a bed with all my sisters. I had been given a new bed, made out of bamboo by my uncle, with enough room for my sister and me, and there was even a brand new air fan standing in the corner. At the side of the room was a small cupboard where my clothes from Hong Kong were now hanging. My sister had done the unpacking and had taken great pleasure in seeing the new clothes and underwear I had brought back. She even tried on one or two of the dresses. As I lay there in the bed that night with my sister's arm around me and her warm body snuggled next to mine, I truly felt at home.

The next day relatives and friends arrived to welcome me back. Some of my old school friends dropped in to see how I was. One or two of them said that they too might be going to Hong Kong soon as there was no work available and money was as usual scarce. I told them it was hard work and not all fun but there were good times to be had. Even as I spoke I realised these were exactly the same stories I had heard, back when thoughts of me going to Hong Kong were still only a distant possibility.

As the days turned into weeks and I settled back down I started to think about what I had done in the last year or so and what I could do now. I had started to make plans for my future while I was in Hong Kong but there was no urgency. I would take my time and enjoy my freedom for a while. I had done my bit for the family, knowing now my younger sisters would not have to do the same. They would never know the sacrifices I had made for I could never tell them. For the time being I would relax and just enjoy being home again.

14. Recipe

4 Cups of Love	1 Cup of Friendship
2 Cups of Loyalty	5 Cups of Hope
4 Quarts of Faith	1 Barrel of Laughter
2 Spoons of Tenderness	3 Cups of Forgiveness

Take Love and Loyalty. Mix thoroughly with Faith. Blend with Tenderness (adding a drop of Kindness and Understanding). Add Friendship and Hope. Sprinkle abundantly with Laughter. Make it with sunshine. Serve daily with generous helpings of Forgiveness.

(Plate engraving taken from grandmother's kitchen)

SO HERE I SIT on the little wooden bench outside my father's house. The bench is still the same. The tree providing shade is taller and the house is a little larger with the addition. We still do not have a toilet that flushes but that is not a luxury to me any more. As a kind of compromise we have drilled a well and placed a hand pump inside the kitchen, so at least we do not queue up outside at the communal pump for our water. My younger brothers and sisters continue to share the beds but it is not as cramped as it used to be. So I guess you could say that in small ways our lives have improved.

* * *

Sheena is on her third tour in Hong Kong. We continue to write from time to time, and even though I don't want to hear every detail about Hong Kong including the mamas and the bar scene, she often provides bits of gossip. She says she is still looking for "Mr Right". From her letters you can tell she is as strong as ever but after her "bad customer" experience, which will always be with her, she is very careful who she goes out with. Her letters bring back both the sad and the good times and it does no harm to reflect on them occasionally. Will she ever settle down? I don't know. I would like to think that the right guy will one day come along. She certainly deserves it. Her family has prospered from her work. They have a very nice house and some land, which they farm, and I read in her last letter that she was buying her father a secondhand car. The only disturbing news was that her younger sister was soon to join her in Hong Kong. I felt sad when I read it but at least she has Sheena there to protect her.

It took Baby a long time to settle down. She even considered going to Japan to work the bars there but changed her mind. She found herself what she said was a nice boyfriend who had a good job with the airforce, and they put themselves on a list to be allocated a small house near the BASA military air base. I went to her wedding as a bridesmaid. Sheena unfortunately could not be there as she was already back in Hong Kong, but we did send her some of the photographs. Baby and her husband settled down to married life and were planning to start a family, which is why her last letter came as a bit of a shock. After only six months they have separated. She wrote that once they had settled down all they seemed to do was argue. There is no divorce among Catholics in the Philippines and she has moved back with her parents. She finished her letter saying she has decided to return to Hong Kong. The promotion has confirmed that she will be allowed to work in the same bar as Sheena.

Mika has married since her return and managed to get a job, of all places in McDonald's at San Fernando. Her husband is an auto mechanic. They have built a small house next door to her parents and she seems to have found true love. If any of us girls deserves happiness, it has to be Mika. After all that she went through both before and during Hong Kong, I thought that she would lose it all and just fall into an abyss. But she has regained control of her life. To look at her you would think she was another ordinary girl settling down to married life. Her husband—I have met him on a few occasions—treats her like a jewel, never leaving her side unless it is absolutely necessary. Their only drop of sadness is that they are desperate to have a baby of their own. But of course, with Mika's insides, that is not possible. The last I heard was that they were going to adopt and have already started making enquiries. I am sure there will be plenty of babies to choose from. Mika insists that it must be a little boy and

I think I know why. She is already planning for the event and has asked Baby and me to be godparents.

As for Edna, she is still around. I bumped into her one day in San Fernando. She has put on even more weight and still works with the promotion. She stopped and passed a few pleasantries, asking me how I was and what was I doing. She said we were one of her best groups and parted by giving me a small kiss on the cheek. How strange. She was instrumental in our going to Hong Kong and I am sure she knew at the outset what would be in store for us, yet she just did her job. I do not resent her. In fact, I could not help laughing quietly as I watched her walk away. She was wearing a jacket, probably from Hong Kong, with a Chinese dragon embroidered on the back. It crossed my mind that Sheena may have sent it to her.

Roseanna put Hong Kong behind her and went as planned with the promotion to Canada. She knew she would be expected to strip and dance naked but as she said to me before, "It can't be any worse than what we were expected to do in Hong Kong." I guess she is right. Even though there is no nudity in Hong Kong, once you have gone out a few times the shyness and embarrassment of undressing in front of a stranger soon disappears. And as she said, "There is a lot more money to be earned." Last I heard, she had married a Canadian guy and is expecting their first baby. I am sure that this is another reason why so many other girls allow themselves to go through this. Maybe for them, they dream, there will be a happy ending too.

My eldest sister is now married and has a three-year-old son. She spends all her time with him. Her husband is a sweet and gentle man who works hard to provide for his family. He has a steady job with the local council. Since the eruption of Mount Pinatubo and the devastation caused by lahar flows, many previously unemployed men have found jobs clearing the roads of lahar and building dikes to prevent further damage. It does not pay much and it is hard and dirty work with sometimes long hours, but it is a job. They have been able to build a small house and buy a few chickens so their prospects are looking brighter. She often visits us on Sunday. When we accompany our mother to church, returning home to share a family meal, I watch her with Denny, her son, and can see that she is pouring so much love into him. We never talk about her other child. I am sure it still hurts her but I know that Denny will never want for anything, least of all the love of his mother. The father of her first child, our family friend, was killed in a road accident in Saudi Arabia while I was in Hong Kong. I feel sad for his widowed wife and their four children, who must now grow up without a father. The terrible secret that we had feared might one day slip out was buried with him. I was not there but I was told that my mother, father and eldest sister attended his funeral once the body had been flown home.

My mother and father are pretty much the same. If anything, my mother now has more say in family matters. She is really proud of her grandchildren and spends as much time as she can with them. Though I never told her all of my experiences I am sure she noticed I came back a different person. I can feel it when she gives me a hug. The whole Hong Kong episode has brought us closer together.

I was able to buy a jeepney for my father. By using it as a taxi, he supplements his earnings from the farm. I never talked in any detail with my father about Hong Kong. He was closest to the promotion managers, and if anybody knew what went on, he did. But even with everything that happened, I can't blame him. He is my father and he will always have my love. My younger brothers and sisters are a little bit bigger and every bit as noisy. I remember when I first returned—for days they would not leave me alone. The little one kept asking if I was going away again. I constantly told her *no*. Then she would throw her thin arms around me, saying *I don't want you to leave us again.*

As for me, I can say that now I have some of the strength of Sheena and much of the sensitivity of Baby. I am older, wiser and still a little philosophical. I have married and have a daughter of my own named Grace. My husband and I are even talking about having another one. I have opened a small shop and my sister and I work it together. Half of it is simply selling the basic requirements of life—rice, eggs and other foodstuffs. The other half is devoted to clothes. I have an arrangement with Sheena and the girls under her wing. Whenever they return from Hong Kong they bring back tee shirts and other bargains. Especially those clothes that are almost constantly on sale in such shops as Giordano, Bossini and G2000.

I watch the young girls as they slide their hands through the clothes on the rail. I make a point of not having anything hanging up on rusty nails and I watch them as they take hold of each one and measure it against their body as they gaze into the mirror. I can't help but wonder if they are wishing for the same things I wished for at their age: that I had a purse full of money and that I could buy something new. How many of them will turn out to be another Mary I don't know, but every time I see one leave my shop I say a little prayer to the Lord that if this is to be their fate he will give them a Sheena or a Baby to accompany them.

One day, while sitting on the bench sipping orange juice and watching Grace playing with the other children, a young girl unexpectedly sat down. I had seen her around the shop from time to time. I paused and put down my pen.

"Excuse me, Ate," she said, using the common greeting of children in the Philippines to someone older than themselves.

"You've been to Hong Kong, haven't you?"

I looked into her deep brown eyes and said, "Yes, why do you ask?"

"Well, my father said I can go too, to help earn money for the family."

I saw fear and intrigue in her innocent young eyes and I asked, "How old are you?"

"Fifteen," she said.

With a feeling of shock, I replied, "But they won't let you go to Hong Kong. You're too young."

She twisted the handkerchief she was holding around her fingers. Then she said, "My father said that if we wait six months the man at the promotion could use a dance card from one of the other girls to send me. All I need is a passport with a higher age on it."

I did not really know what to say. It appeared that her father had already made plans for her. And my mind flashed to the talk I had had with my father on that same bench about the very same subject.

"Do you want to go?" I asked her.

"Well, we don't have much money, my mother is pregnant again and I am the eldest. I just want to help them."

I looked into her eyes again, seeing a flicker of myself. The innocence of her reply made me remember all the stories I had heard in the past from the other girls when we asked each other about Hong Kong.

"That's why I wanted to ask you—what is it like?"

I took hold of her arms first, and then realised that my firm grip was hurting her.

"I'm sorry," I said, relaxing my grip. "It's just that—" I started to explain but couldn't. I searched my mind and soul for something I could say to convince this little thing that going overseas was not for her. But what good would it do? Would it prevent her from being sent there? Probably not. I realised that nothing I could say in the next few minutes would prevent this sweet child from leaving her home. But I had to say something.

"All I can say, child, is that it is very hard work, both before you get to Hong Kong and when you are there. There are a lot of people who will try and take advantage of you."

I was trying to speak and listen to myself at the same time.

"If you go I hope you will find some new friends who will help you stand up and overcome the problems you will find there." The faces of Sheena and Baby appeared in my mind.

"But one thing to remember: even though they will tell you that you are only going to dance, do not believe them."

I paused and searched her face. There was no smile, no frown, just a sweet, young, innocent face waiting for me to finish. I took a deep breath.

"Even though they say you will only dance," I said, knowing I must continue, "there will come a time when you will be forced, by one means or another, to go out and sleep with the customers."

There, I thought, I've said it.

"Do you mean, have sex with them?"

Her simple reply, the way she said it, left me a little shocked.

"Yes," I replied.

She carried on: "Other than that, is it a nice place?"

I thought she had not heard me or did not understand what sleeping with customers meant, so I repeated myself, this time with even more force. "Didn't you hear what I said?"

She did not reply but waited for something more.

"Yes, Hong Kong can be a nice place if you're lucky and have nice friends, but you will be expected to sleep, have sex with men, sometimes lots of different men." I stopped and released my grip as she stood up. I had no words left to offer.

"Oh, Ate, I'm not a virgin," she said sheepishly.

"What!" I blurted.

"My uncle took my cherry last year."

Stunned, I could only look at her. She turned and started to walk away. Then she turned back and said, "Thank you, Ate."

I watched her thin, childlike body for a second, then said, "Sorry, child, what's your name?"

"Marie," she said.

Then with a half-walk and a half-skip, she disappeared down the road.

Glossary

amah: Domestic helper; nanny.

Ate: A form of address used by children in the Philippines to address older female companions. May be translated as "auntie" or "big sister".

bagoong: Salted and fermented fish paste made from shrimp or fish.

bar fine: A type of "escort fee" representing the price paid in order to "buy a girl out of a bar", usually for a single evening.

barrio: Neighbourhood or village community.

BASA: A Philippine-run military base located in Northern Luzon.

cherry: A term used in Asia to describe a girl's virginity. Other colloquial but non-derogatory expressions include "cherry girl" or "a girl's cherry".

Christos: Men at a *sabong* (cockfight) who place bets on behalf of individuals or small groups of people.

CR: Comfort room. Also bathroom or restroom.

Filipina: Filipino of female gender.

Filipino: A native of the Philippines (male or female).

go-go bar: A bar where girls dance, usually in bathing suits or one- or two-piece costumes, and which is run by one or more female floor managers called mamasans. The stage of a go-go bar typically features a series of vertically mounted chrome poles around which girls dance.

jeepney: A common form of bus-like transportation in the Philippines. A jeepney is essentially a jeep with an adjoining passenger section capable of holding approximately a dozen passengers. Jeepneys are renowned for their artistic exteriors.

Kai Tak International Airport: Hong Kong's original international airport located in Kowloon which was closed in 1998 in conjunction with the opening of the present-day Chek Lap Kok International Airport located on Hong Kong's Lantau Island.

ladies' drink: An expensive drink, often non-alcoholic, which a customer may choose to buy for a girl working in a go-go bar, karaoke or nightclub.

lahar: Volcanic ash (mixed with water) left over from the Mount Pinatubo eruption of June 12, 1991, which resulted in the closure of Clark Air Base in Angeles, Philippines.

mamasan: A floor manageress of a go-go bar or nightclub. Go-go bars often have two or three mamasans working at one bar. Also, mama.

MTR: Mass Transit Railway, Hong Kong's subway system.

Pampanga: A province in northern Philippines located a few hours' drive from Manila. Its capital is San Fernando. Other well-known cities in Pampanga include Angeles City and Tarlac.

pec-pec: Tagalog for vagina.

peso: The currency of the Philippines.

Pilipino: The official language of the Philippines.

promotion: An organisation in the Philippines that trains girls, particularly in dance techniques, for the purpose of going overseas to work in bars.

province: A term used to describe those regions outside of metropolitan Manila including any of the Philippine provinces, particularly those in Northern Luzon and the Visayas.

sabong: Tagalog for cockfight, a popular male sporting event in the Philippines.

short-time session: Buying a girl out of the bar for less than one full night and for less than the full price of a bar fine.

tab: Check or bill, especially one with a running total.

Tagalog: The principal regional dialect of the Philippines as spoken in Manila and its surrounding areas.

titi: Tagalog for penis.

triad: A Chinese Mafia organisation with roots in Hong Kong.

tricycle/trike: A three-wheeled motorised vehicle with a sidecar used to carry one or two sitting passengers.